Was she r[eady to face] her husb[and? Still in] her funeral clothes, and with Leo expecting her to walk down an aisle?

In spite of how he'd rejected her before, she couldn't deny that she'd still had dreams... She shook her head to dislodge the humiliating reminder of the pull he'd had over her.

"Wait..."

He arched a dark brow. "You thought I didn't mean it? Don't you remember that I don't bluff?"

No, he didn't bluff. He obviously meant to go through with this outrageous act. And suddenly Angelica was somewhere between past and present, her body humming to be close to this man again, humming in a way that told her she hadn't gotten over him at all. *Physically*, she told herself desperately. Emotionally, he could never hurt her again.

She pulled her arm free of his loose grip. "Are you kidnapping me all the way to the altar, Leo?"

He took a step back. "You're free to go. But I can assure you that marrying me will be so much easier and efficient in the long term."

Irish author **Abby Green** ended a very glamorous career in film and TV—which really consisted of a lot of standing in the rain outside actors' trailers—to pursue her love of romance. After she'd bombarded Harlequin with manuscripts, they kindly accepted one, and an author was born. She lives in Dublin, Ireland, and loves any excuse for distraction. Visit abby-green.com or email abbygreenauthor@gmail.com.

Books by Abby Green

Harlequin Presents

His Housekeeper's Twin Baby Confession
Heir for His Empire
"I Do" for Revenge
Rush to the Altar
Billion-Dollar Baby Shock

Princess Brides for Royal Brothers

Mistaken as His Royal Bride

Hot Winter Escapes

Claimed by the Crown Prince

Brazilian Billionaire Brothers

The Heir Dilemma
On His Bride's Terms

Visit the Author Profile page
at Harlequin.com for more titles.

BRIDE OF BETRAYAL

ABBY GREEN

Harlequin
PRESENTS

If you purchased this book without a cover you should be aware that this book is stolen property. It was reported as "unsold and destroyed" to the publisher, and neither the author nor the publisher has received any payment for this "stripped book."

MIX
Paper | Supporting responsible forestry
FSC® C021394

Harlequin® PRESENTS™

Recycling programs for this product may not exist in your area.

ISBN-13: 978-1-335-21337-2

Bride of Betrayal

Copyright © 2025 by Abby Green

All rights reserved. No part of this book may be used or reproduced in any manner whatsoever without written permission.

Without limiting the author's and publisher's exclusive rights, any unauthorized use of this publication to train generative artificial intelligence (AI) technologies is expressly prohibited.

This is a work of fiction. Names, characters, places and incidents are either the product of the author's imagination or are used fictitiously. Any resemblance to actual persons, living or dead, businesses, companies, events or locales is entirely coincidental.

For questions and comments about the quality of this book, please contact us at CustomerService@Harlequin.com.

TM and ® are trademarks of Harlequin Enterprises ULC.

Harlequin Enterprises ULC
22 Adelaide St. West, 41st Floor
Toronto, Ontario M5H 4E3, Canada
www.Harlequin.com

HarperCollins Publishers
Macken House, 39/40 Mayor Street Upper,
Dublin 1, D01 C9W8, Ireland
www.HarperCollins.com

Printed in Lithuania

BRIDE OF BETRAYAL

PROLOGUE

Rome

LEONARDO FALZONE STOOD against the car, the folded arms and nonchalance of his stance giving no indication as to the thrumming tension in his tall, powerful body. The other drivers looked sideways at him, as if sensing there wasn't something quite right about this particular chauffeur. Even though he wore a uniform and a hat, the clothes looked somehow...*wrong*.

And they'd be right, because Leo Falzone was no mere chauffeur, even if he had been hired—under a different name—to help ferry the guests away from the funeral of the man who had betrayed him heinously, taking advantage of a friendship that had been forged in the foster-care system.

A friendship Leo had believed to be as solid as a rock, until his friend and business partner had betrayed him not only professionally but also personally.

Except, Leo couldn't exactly blame Aldo Bianchi for the personal betrayal. After all, Leo's lover had chosen to turn her affections to Aldo, no doubt seduced by his promises to make her a rich woman.

Rich from the years that Leo had spent sweating and toiling to create Falzone Industries.

You rejected her first. His conscience pricked. Yes, he had sent her away because she'd been saying nonsense, about loving him. He hadn't asked for her love. He wasn't in the market for that. So he'd told her to leave. And then she'd gone straight into his best friend's bed.

Aldo had been his business partner, but they'd both known that Leo was the brains behind the company. Leo had thought Aldo was happy playing to his skills, utilising his social charm to bring in business and create financial partnerships, but Leo had underestimated just how jealous and bitter his friend had really been.

Aldo's sense of injustice had grown along with his drug addiction, something Leo had failed to notice, much to his regret. Leo had only realised the full extent of the disaster that had unfolded when he'd had time to figure it all out in jail, where he'd spent the last three years. Accused of embezzlement and insider trading, by his closest ally. Set up and arrested before he'd had time to even get his wits together.

Aldo had demonstrated all too well that, in spite of his laissez-faire attitude to working, he had somehow managed to frame Leo so comprehensively that it had taken three years to prove his innocence. And in the meantime, Aldo had been at the helm of Falzone Industries—renamed Bianchi Industries.

Not only that, he'd married Leo's ex-lover, a mere month after they'd split, demonstrating how little Leo had really known her. And her real agenda all along—to feather her nest.

Leo's sentencing and incarceration had coincided with the news that Aldo Bianchi and his stunning wife had just bought a sumptuous holiday home in Sicily.

On his recent release from jail, Leo's desire to seek revenge on his ex-friend had been thwarted when Aldo Bianchi had been found dead a week ago. He'd died of an overdose, in an alleyway behind one of Rome's most famous nightclubs.

Leo's mouth firmed. Maybe it had been Aldo's guilty conscience that had pushed his drug-taking to dangerous levels, but more likely not. It had been the success of the company, which had thrived in the last three years—purely because of the way Leo had set things up. It couldn't have failed to succeed. No doubt another consideration by his friend when timing Leo's fall from grace.

But now Aldo was dead, depriving Leo of any sense of catharsis or revenge. But there was someone else in this equation. Someone who had arguably betrayed Leo even more heinously. Because she'd been the one who had lain in his bed and whispered lies into his ear. Had she been scheming with Aldo while she was with Leo? He couldn't rule it out. In any case, she'd gone straight to Aldo and destroyed Leo's life's work and reputation by helping to put him in jail for a fraud he'd never committed.

Three years he'd spent in that stinking place, until his legal team had finally managed to prove his innocence.

Now, he wanted to regain full control of his company again, put it back into his name, and all that stood in his way of achieving that goal was the woman who had inherited Aldo's share of the business. His duplicitous grieving widow.

The woman standing alone by the grave was a tall, still figure. Dressed in black, in a dress that on the surface looked demure—lace overlaid silk covered her from neck to wrist to knee, but it clung to her figure showcasing a classic womanly shape. High full breasts, narrow waist flaring out to her hips, and endlessly long legs. Feet encased in high, sharp heels. Thick, dark hair pulled back into a low bun.

A short veil hid her beautiful, treacherous face. A face that had haunted Leo for years. Three years to be precise. Green/golden eyes. Finely etched brows. Straight nose. High cheekbones, a delicate but defined jaw. A wide, lush mouth made for—*Basta!* Leo shut down his rapidly unravelling thoughts.

She did not affect him. Not any more. He had plans to regain control of his business and at the same time rehabilitate his damaged image. And for that, he needed not only the other half of his business, but also a wife.

And not just any wife. A wife who would understand that he had no desire for a *real* wife. A wife who would perform her duties in public but keep her distance in private. A wife who would hand over what he was owed.

After watching his entire family be gunned down by a Mafia thug in front of him as a young boy, Leo had never harboured any desire to risk inflicting such a horror on a child. He didn't want a family. He'd *had* a happy family, parents, brothers, and it had all been wiped out in a few hellish minutes, instilling within him a deep primal fear of ever having that and losing that again. He'd only survived because his mother had shoved him behind a cabinet.

No, all he needed was a temporary wife and there was only one woman in the world who could perfom this duty for him.

His blood roared. The woman standing by the graveside was about to pay for her sins…by becoming Angelica Falzone.

CHAPTER ONE

FREE. AT LAST. Angelica wanted to rip off the net veil that covered her face, and throw it aside, tip her head back and let the rays of the sun blast all the way through her, incinerating the last three years of purgatory, cleansing her of the toxicity she'd had to endure.

Cleansing her of the cynical shell she'd had to build around herself to survive. Not just the sham marriage she'd never wanted, but also the pain of the earlier rejection she'd suffered at the hands of her first lover. And love. Who she'd thought had loved her. When she'd told him she loved him he'd turned arctic and told her to leave. Now she cursed the day they'd ever met.

She'd felt like such a naive fool. She'd fallen for the first man she'd slept with. She'd been mortified. She'd grown up on the edges of the systemic Mafia violence and crime in Sicily and she'd considered herself tough and street smart, yet out in the big world, she'd realised that she was as vulnerable as the next woman.

She'd been twenty-one and now she was twenty-four but sometimes she felt much, much older.

But three years ago, her lover had shown her that she'd still retained innocence and hope, even after seeing so much and losing her father to a violent murder by the criminal gangs who'd embroiled him reluctantly in their criminal activities.

That had made her lover's rejection even worse, the fact that he'd not only taken her innocence, literally, but also destroyed her nascent hope for a life not blighted by violence. A life that could contain the ordinary, yet extraordinary pleasures of normality like having a family and not living in fear for their lives.

In a way she was glad she'd learnt that lesson, harsh as it had been, because she could move on with her life, and know what to expect. And being free was enough for now. She didn't need anything more.

She only had to walk away from this grave and get to the car, instruct the driver where to take her and then…she could finally rip it all off. The veil hiding her lack of grief. The custom-made Dolce & Gabbana dress. The outward display of wealth that had hidden so much.

'Signora Bianchi, your car is over here.'

She nodded at one of the funeral directors and said *grazie*, turning from the grave to follow him. She felt like telling him not to call her *Bianchi*, she was free of that hated name now. But she held her tongue. He led her over to where a driver was standing by a car. He opened the back door.

Angelica lifted her face slightly from where she'd been looking at the ground, as much to watch her step in the vertiginous heels as to avoid eye contact with anyone.

The driver was tall, tall enough to send a tiny frisson of *something* down her spine. She lifted her head a little more but the sun was in her face and she couldn't make out much more than his height and broad shoulders. His cap was pulled low.

She told herself she was being ridiculous. For the first year of her marriage she'd thought she'd seen her ex-lover everywhere but of course she hadn't because he was in jail. Incarcerated because of his business partner Aldo's greed and jealousy. As much as she'd known he hadn't deserved it, she'd been in a jail of her own, albeit a gilded one, so they'd both been punished for their ill-fated association with each other, and Aldo. Did that make them even? She wasn't sure. But what she was sure of was that she never wanted to see him again, and she was pretty certain he wouldn't want to see her either. Not after that brutal break-up and everything that had ensued.

Leonardo Falzone undoubtedly wouldn't understand why on earth she would have gone from him to his best friend. He'd see it as a betrayal even if he had been the one to dump her. Aldo hadn't missed the opportunity to stick the knife in even deeper. It hadn't been enough to steal his friend's business and get him locked up on false charges, he'd had to steal his lover. But even when Angelica had tried to tell Aldo that it would mean nothing because Leonardo hadn't felt anything for her, Aldo hadn't listened.

She knew that Leonardo had been released from

prison because the press had been full of it, but there had been no sign of him coming to collect his dues. Angelica was sure that it was the news of his nemesis's release that had pushed Aldo over the edge, making him even more volatile than usual. Hence his overdose. A sad, pitiful end to a sad, pitiful human being.

Time to move on, finally. She stopped just before stepping into the car and lifted her face slightly and said, 'Straight to the airport, please.'

She was aware of the driver dipping his head to indicate he'd heard her and then she was in the back of the car, in the dark cool interior. The privacy division between her and the driver was up, so she couldn't see him walk around the car. She breathed a sigh of relief and finally yanked off the veil. She wasn't even taking a suitcase with her. All she needed was her passport. She was leaving everything behind.

She pulled the pins out of her hair and loosened it, wincing a little with relief. She also kicked off the shoes, stretching out her pinched toes.

She put her head back against the seat and felt tension slowly draining out of her body as the car moved away from the graveyard in central Rome and out into the city.

She was exhausted. She wanted to sleep for a month. At least. And then—she lifted her head when she saw a sign indicating a turn for the airport. A turn the driver didn't take.

Another turn-off for the airport approached and again the driver sailed past. Angelica sat up straight.

Tension flooded her body and something that had been familiar for three years now, and constant. Fear.

She leaned forward and knocked on the privacy window. No response. She knocked again. No response. The fear churned and turned to panic. She tried the door of the car. Locked. It wasn't as if she could hurl herself from a car that was speeding into the outskirts of Rome. She hadn't survived the last three years to fall at the final hurdle.

And then anger started to rise, eclipsing the panic, and she welcomed it. She *knew* she was safe from harm now. Aldo was gone and anyone in league with him had scuttled back under whatever rock they'd come from, and good riddance. If she'd had any doubt otherwise she would have been much more circumspect today.

So there was no one who could possibly want to harm her—her blood ran cold. The driver. Tall, broad shoulders. Angelica shook her head as if that might clear it of the ridiculous notion that perhaps it could be— At that precise moment the privacy division slid down a few inches.

The driver had taken off the cap and Angelica could see the top half of his face. It took a second for her mind to compute what she was seeing. A broad forehead. Thick dark hair. Messy. But it was those eyes, under dark slashing brows. *His eyes.* Indelibly burnt onto her brain, and into her memory.

Dark. Dark as the night. It was only when you got really close that it was possible to make out lighter hints of gold. And she'd been as close as one could get. She'd drowned in those golden lights.

She breathed out his name as if she had to say it out loud to be sure. 'Leonardo Falzone.'

Those eyes flicked to the road and then back. 'Ciao, *Angel*.'

Angelica went cold. If she'd been in any doubt that this man was who she thought he was, it was removed. *Angel*. He was the only one who used to call her that.

'Don't call me that.'

His eyes were on the road now. Hard, obsidian. 'You used to like it.'

A memory flash of two bodies, sweat-slicked, joined as one, straining to reach the pinnacle, hearts pounding, ecstasy just out of reach, and him, this man, reaching his hand down between their bodies to touch her, saying, *'Come for me, Angel, I need you to—'*

Angelica snapped, 'I used to like a lot of things. What are you doing here? Where are we going?'

Her heart was pounding now. Not out of fear. Even in this situation, Angelica wasn't scared. She knew that no matter what had happened between them, this man wouldn't hurt her. Physically. It suddenly struck her that she'd just spent three years with a man where the threat of violence hung in the air like a noxious perfume, but who could never have really harmed her because he never had access to that deepest most secret part of her.

The ways he'd had to harm her had been external. Through the people she loved.

But this man who was now driving her to some unknown location, he'd had the power to decimate her. And he already had. But she'd survived. He no longer had that power and never would again.

He asked mockingly, 'You're not going to congratulate me on my exoneration of a crime I didn't commit? On my freedom?'

A guilt that wasn't hers made her insides cramp a little. 'I know you didn't deserve what Aldo did to you.'

His eyes met hers through the mirror and she shivered. No gold in those eyes today. Just endless dark depths. 'And yet you did nothing to stop it, or defend me. You were in on it with him, obviously.'

He did believe she'd betrayed him, as she'd feared.

No, she hadn't done anything, because she couldn't. She'd had nothing to do with it but Aldo had made sure she was implicated by forcing her into a relationship. Not that this man would listen to her. Not that she could tell him. She still had too much at stake. Too much to protect. If there had ever been a time when she would have confided in this man, it had long gone.

She asked, 'Where are you taking me?'

He just said enigmatically, 'You'll soon see,' and the privacy window slid back up. Angelica sat back, folding her arms tight across her chest. She was reeling. She hadn't expected this. She'd never expected to see Leonardo Falzone again. *Really?* asked a small voice. *Didn't you dream of him? Dream of him telling you, 'I love you too' after you'd blurted out how you felt?*

Angelica's lips pressed together, as if that could

help block out the memory of the horror-struck look on his face when she'd told him she loved him three years ago. She'd been so wrong. She'd read emotion into his desire for her but it had just been physical. And, to give him his due, he'd never promised anything other than that. There'd been no talk of a future, or feelings. Just a mutual fascination, bonding over a shared background, both growing up in different parts of Sicily. Both blighted by the violence endemic in that society. Both of their lives ripped asunder because of it. And then there had been the mutual combustible chemistry. Like nothing she'd ever experienced. *Or ever would again,* whispered a voice. She ignored it. It still mortified her to think she'd fallen for her first lover. More fool her.

Leonardo had lost his entire family right in front of his eyes. A horror he'd told her about one night in bed, in a suspiciously dispassionate voice. She'd told him about losing her father, who'd been on the periphery of the Mafia violence but not peripheral enough. She'd told him about being scouted by a modelling agency and how that had helped her to get away from Sicily.

And not just her, her mother and younger brother. Her brother had already been in danger of aggravating the local Mafia gangs by the time she'd had enough money to set them up in a new place, far away from Sicily to protect them from any chance that the same people who'd killed her father might consider them to be too risky to stay alive. Her brother had been angry and disillusioned after the death of his father. Angelica had seen too many young people fall foul of the gangs and her brother had had good reason to antagonise them, which would have only put them in the crosshairs of danger.

It had taken all of Angelica's and her mother's fortitude to make him see that he would have to let it go and move on with his own life.

She'd been advised not to tell anyone about their new whereabouts, to almost treat them as if they were in a witness protection programme, for fear that anyone from their past would try to contact them or expose their location, and so Angelica had remained vigilant, telling no one, not even her lover. Even though she'd wanted to.

And, after growing up in a society where silence about criminal activity was ingrained in your blood, it had been terrifying to think of trusting another with their safety. It had led her to keeping herself to herself, while working, avoiding close friendships or relationships. Leonardo had been the first person to sneak under her guard and he'd done it before she could pull the drawbridge back up.

She'd almost told him about them so many times, but she'd always held back at the last moment. Their affair had been so whirlwind, literally just a few weeks. She was going to tell him on the day that she'd told him she loved him, feeling as if she could trust him with her most precious secret, but he'd rejected her and it had been one consolation at least that she hadn't spilled everything to him.

Not that that had kept her family safe, because Aldo Bianchi, Leonardo's business partner, had somehow found out about her mother and brother and their whereabouts, even though she didn't live with them, and had taken huge care to always protect their new lives.

He'd then used that information to blackmail her into marriage, demonstrating the terrifying reach of the Sicilian gangs. By then her brother had been about to do his final year school exams. They'd been happy, settled. He'd been talking about university courses he wanted to do. He no longer talked about seeking justice or vengeance for their father, but Aldo had threatened all of that, telling Angelica it would only take one phone call for her father's killers to come and finish the job.

Aldo had grown up in a foster home with Leonardo. He too had been a part of that toxic violence, but where Leonardo had cut all ties with anyone from his past, Aldo had assured her that he still had contacts. He'd shown her a video of her brother, going to school. Laughing. Messing. Being a carefree young man. And her mother—shopping. Doing mundane tasks. Also happy.

The terrifying knowledge that he had someone close enough to put her mother and brother under surveillance had meant she had no choice but to comply. This wasn't a situation where she could go to the police. This was a threat that operated on a far more dangerous and insidious level.

Angelica dragged her mind back from things she couldn't change. So what did Leonardo want now? Revenge was the most obvious thing. And now that

Aldo was gone, clearly all the blame was to be lain at her feet.

She'd been wrong to believe Leonardo when he'd told her that he had no interest in living under the yoke of the cycle of violence and retribution of their forbears. Clearly, he was no different, seeking his vengeance. And yet...could she really blame him? She couldn't even begin to imagine what he might have been through while in prison.

She pushed aside any hint of remorse or sympathy. It was because of her association with this man that she too had suffered, and her family had been in danger.

She cultivated the rising tide of anger, anything to distract her from the far more disturbing emotions making her chest tight.

Leo had to try and control the tumult in his gut, but Angelica's scent lingered, even now with a privacy window between them. That distinctive scent of gardenia mixed with something much earthier. It had instantly evoked a slew of images in his head—seeing her for the first time at that function in Rome. Reeling at her beauty.

The first kiss. The first touch. The first time he'd seen her naked, and put his hand to her flesh, feeling as if he were tainting her. He'd been her first lover... or had he? That had tortured him in recent years, the idea that she'd feigned her innocence while laughing at him behind his back for his romantic gullibility.

Leo shut out the memories. She *was* tainted now,

by her relationship with his ex-business partner, but he had no intention of ever touching her again. He just needed her presence.

Before sitting into the car, when she'd lifted her face briefly and he'd seen the familiar lush outline of her mouth, it had taken all of his strength not to haul her into him and crush it beneath his. Driven by anger, *not* desire, he told himself now. But his hands clasped the steering wheel tightly betraying that inner turmoil.

He shouldn't have come here. He'd had no choice. She'd haunted him for three years of torturous incarceration.

There was unfinished business between him and Angelica Malgeri. Angelica Bianchi. Soon to be Angelica Falzone. Leo's mouth tipped up into a mirthless smile as he saw the steeple of the chapel appear in the distance. After all, wasn't this what ran in his blood, in spite of everything, handed down from generations? The need for vengeance?

This woman had proven to him that he was no better than his ancestors, in spite of his attempts to pretend otherwise, and all he could do now was lean into that need and exorcise her from his system for good. He would have no peace until she'd paid her dues.

Angelica was tense as the car slowed and came to a stop outside a small church. Ornate. Old. Forbidding with its time-mottled walls and crumbling religious statues. She could see a small cluster of men in suits near the entrance. Her heart beat loudly. What was going on?

Leonardo got out of the car and came around to open her door. Sunlight blazed into the dark, making her squint. Now that she knew who he was, she couldn't *un*see that formidable build. Tall and powerful. Every muscle taut and honed. And yet even now she could sense something that hadn't been there before. An edge. As if he'd cultivated another layer of steel since she'd seen him last.

Well, so had she. She pushed down the tumult inside her and determined not to let him see how much he'd surprised her. He put out a hand to help her out but she ignored it, taking her time to put back on her shoes before stepping out with as much grace as she could muster.

She regretted undoing her hair and taking off the veil now. Clearly she'd celebrated her freedom too soon. But when she stood up straight she was much closer to Leonardo than she'd anticipated, because he hadn't moved back.

They were practically touching. Even in the heels, her head only came to his shoulder. His scent wrapped around her, mocking her for not noticing it before. Musky and woodsy. Sandalwood. His scent had always made her feel safe and that reminder made her jerk back so suddenly that she would have fallen if he hadn't reached out to take her upper arm in his hand.

His touch was like a bomb detonating inside her, blasting apart the ice that she'd cultivated over three years. The ice was melting and becoming molten faster than she could stop it. She looked up, stunned and dismayed that he could still have this effect on her.

His eyes were golden now, blazing down into hers. Nostrils flaring. Jaw taut. He was the one to let her go and she took a jerky step back, thankfully not falling down.

'What's going on, Leonardo?'

He closed the door of the car and leaned back against it, folding his arms across his chest as if they had all the time in the world. 'No chit-chat? I think after three years where you've lived handsomely off the proceeds of my work you owe me a civil conversation.'

Angelica felt the sun on her head, beating down. Merciless. Like this man. He had definitely changed. Gone was the kindness she'd seen in his eyes and face when they'd first met. It was one of the first things that had attracted her to him—the fact that he didn't appear to have the same air of jaded, brittle ennui as everyone else around them. He'd still had an almost childlike enthusiasm.

Not any more. He was as hardened as everyone else. And no wonder. He'd been in jail. She swallowed. 'What do you want?'

He tipped his head on one side as if considering. 'Well, for a start, it would have been satisfying to look Aldo in the eye and make him tell me why he set me up.'

She'd known why. Aldo's jealousy for Leonardo's success had turned into something toxic and bitter.

Leonardo went on, 'But he denied me that by dying.'

'You've been fully exonerated,' she pointed out, as if that could make up for what had happened.

'The least that I'm due. I've lost three years of my life.'

So have I, Angelica responded silently.

'You've been busy.'

Angelica blinked. Her work was the only thing that Aldo hadn't sought to control because he'd liked the kudos of being married to one of the world's top models too much. It had probably saved her life.

'Yes, I have.' This year alone she'd traversed the globe more times than she could count. And she was weary. Weary of the travelling and the work. She'd used it as a shield for the last three years but the truth was that she wanted out. And she wanted so much more. To spend time with her family. To see them with her own eyes. Touch them. Talk to them. Aldo hadn't allowed her to visit them, threatening them if she did.

She hadn't seen them now for four years. Her brother had almost finished his university course. Angelica was so proud of him. And in a few hours she would finally have her longed-for reunion.

She lifted her wrist and looked at her watch, panic solidifying in the pit of her belly. She looked at Leonardo. 'I have to be at the airport now or I'll miss my flight.'

He arched a brow. 'Going somewhere nice?'

'It's none of your business.'

'I think it is actually.'

Angelica's heart palpitated. 'Why is that?'

He straightened up from the car and unfolded his arms. 'Because you've got something far more important to attend to.'

Tension spiralled inside her, making her voice sharp, and she spoke without thinking using the shortened version of his name. 'Stop these riddles, Leo, and tell me what's going on.'

His eyes flashed. Angelica cursed her lapse of judgment. *Leo* had been a term of endearment.

But now he was speaking. 'I'll tell you what's going on. There's a local legal official inside that church, vested with the power to marry us. You, Angelica Malgeri, are going to marry me and become my wife until such time as I feel like I've got all the retribution and rehabilitation I need out of our relationship.'

CHAPTER TWO

ANGELICA HAD GONE very still. She looked up at Leo, unblinking, her face pale and set in an expression of... utter disbelief. He might have enjoyed it if the effect of her calling him *Leo* didn't still run through his blood like an electric current. No one else had ever called him that. Not even Aldo.

And then she blinked, long dark luxurious lashes screening those world-famous almond-shaped eyes for a second. Her mouth opened and she said, 'Have you gone quite mad?'

'I've never been more sane.'

'This is the day of my husband's funeral.'

Leo let his mouth quirk up on one side even though he wasn't feeling remotely humorous. 'I can't deny that I do find that quite satisfying.'

'It's not possible.'

There were two spots of colour high in her cheeks now.

'Oh, trust me, it's possible. Once you have the right connections and the funds with which to pay. As you were on your way to the airport you have your passport. That's all the documentation you need. And your hand, to sign the registrar's form.'

Leo knew on a rational level that what he was doing was unorthodox. And ill-advised even. But he was acting on an instinct too strong to ignore. Bring this woman to justice. *His* justice. Make her pay for what she had done. He'd been tortured by nightmares for three years where this woman and a faceless man stood on the other side of the bars and taunted him, before kissing and starting to make love. He always woke up, his body rigid with rejection, pumping with adrenalin, nausea in his gut and a renewed vow that she would pay.

Yet now, she stood before him and he was enacting his revenge and she looked somehow less robust than she had in his nightmares. There was a fragility to her that he didn't remember from before. Dark shadows under her eyes. She looked...somehow older, even though she was still luminously beautiful. As if she carried another layer of...something he couldn't quite define.

Maybe they'd both been shaped by the previous three years except she'd had her freedom and he hadn't.

Angelica took a step back. 'This is crazy. OK, you've had your fun, Leo, I need to get to the airport so can we please leave?' She turned as if to open the car door again but Leo reached out and wrapped his hand around her arm. It felt slim and fragile under his hand, reinforcing a sense of vulnerability. She turned back to face him and he took his arm away and pushed down any such notions.

This woman had gone from his bed to his business partner's and had watched him be hauled off to jail for a crime he didn't commit. She was about as vulnerable as a rhinoceros.

He shook his head, 'You're not going anywhere until you've paid your dues.'

The touch of Leo's hand to her arm lingered, like a brand. She wondered if she was hallucinating. The fact that she was free must have gone to her head and she'd fallen asleep in the back of the car and she would wake up at the airport at any moment...

But no, the sun was still beating down and Leo Falzone was looking at her. Feeling a level of emotion that surprised her, she said, 'I wish we'd never met.'

Leo made a *tsk*'ing sound. 'And lose all those happy memories? We had some good moments, Angel. Unless, of course, you were playacting the whole time, setting the ground for your lover, Aldo.'

Angelica's emotion turned to nausea. 'It wasn't like that.' And much as she hated to admit it now, because everything felt tainted, she and Leo had had good times. The best. Enough to make her believe he was falling in love with her. The anger spiked again and she welcomed it. 'Why on earth would I marry you?'

'You told me you loved me once.'

Angelica's face got hot but before she could respond to that Leo was adding, 'Tell me, were you in league with Aldo for long before we broke up? Or was it the fact that you knew you weren't going to get a commitment from me that drove you into his arms?'

Angelica shuddered inwardly at that image. She'd never been in that man's arms. One saving grace of the last three years.

'I was not in league with anyone.'

'Yet you were married within a month of our break-up.'

Angelica lifted her chin. 'A break-up *you* insisted upon.'

Leo's voice was mocking, 'Are you trying to tell me now that you meant it when you said you loved me?'

Angelica's insides twisted. She had. Not that she'd ever admit that now. 'Don't be ridiculous.'

'So why say it, then? We could have continued as we were, but obviously you were gambling for more.'

She'd said it because it had burst out of her like an unstoppable force. And she'd learnt her lesson. Her heart was cold and hard now. It wouldn't melt again until she saw her family.

'Leo, we have nothing to say to each other, it's all over. Aldo is gone, you're out of jail.'

'And you're still here. Do you really think it'll be so easy to walk away and not face the consequences?'

Angelica went cold inside. 'I've done nothing.'

'Except warm the bed of the man who put me in jail, not to mention colluding with him.'

She got colder. 'There was no collusion.'

'You were married. You inherited his share of *my* company.'

Something eased inside her. Now she knew what the stakes were.

'You can have it. I have no interest in owning any part of your company.'

But he dashed her hope that she could see an end in sight when he said, 'It's not that simple. It would be a long and legally laborious process to transfer your inheritance of his estate to me, but if we were married...it would be a lot simpler.'

'I've had my fill of marriage, I've no intention of getting married again.'

'Sorry to hear that. It wasn't the idyll it appeared to be?'

He didn't sound sorry at all. Angelica clamped her lips together. She'd fallen so hard and so fast for this man that it had taken her totally unawares and she'd almost lost herself entirely, but not before he'd shown her how he really felt. She could never trust him again. They'd spent a heady few weeks together, indulging mostly in the insane chemistry that had sparked between them, she needed to remind herself of that, and that there hadn't been much time for getting to really know one another. It had all been surface level—which she'd subsequently found out was all he had wanted.

'Come to think of it,' he ruminated now, 'you did seem to spend a lot of time apart, so maybe all really wasn't well. Did Aldo's sheen wear off once you realised what a snake he really was?'

Angelica hid behind attack to disguise any hint of

just how flimsy the marriage had been. She raised a brow. 'Reading the gossip columns in jail, were you?'

Now his face flushed but Angelica was too agitated to enjoy it. Her flight would have gone by now. She had to contact her family.

'Look—'

'No, you look.' He cut her off. 'We are not leaving this place until we are man and wife. I want my rightful share of the company back and I need a wife to rehabilitate my image.'

Angelica had heard that steely tone before. She'd heard him speak to adversaries in that tone when they'd been together. And he'd used that tone the day he'd told her to leave, because the relationship was over. Because he had no intention of embarking on a long-term commitment. He hadn't elaborated on that, but Angelica had surmised at the time that the trauma of watching his family be slaughtered had marked him for life. Not that that knowledge had helped her broken heart. It had only made it ache for him and that reminder was like a thorn now.

Worse had been the prospect that it wasn't even trauma holding him back from loving her, but that it was because he just hadn't been that into her.

This man didn't deserve her sympathy. 'You told me the day you kicked me out that you weren't into long-term commitment. What's changed?'

His mouth thinned. 'Unsurprisingly spending time in a prison affords one time to think. But nothing has changed in that regard. This will not be a long-term thing. It'll be marriage in name only—to take back what's mine and to show people that I am settling down, to promote an image of stability and respectability. I can see the merit in that. The business thrived under the image of Aldo's supposed respectability.'

Angelica felt like snorting. Her husband had been anything but respectable. It occurred to her that perhaps this was all a bluster to demonstrate that Leo was serious about getting his due—and Angelica had meant what she'd said, she had no desire to keep Aldo's half of the business. She'd happily sign it over to Leo.

He didn't want to marry her. He couldn't wait to see the back of her three years ago. Maybe if she called his bluff he'd realise how ridiculous this all was. And she couldn't deny the appeal to shake him up a bit—after all, he'd hurt her badly in the past. But that was gone. He didn't affect her any more.

Angelica angled her face up. 'You're right, you know. You didn't deserve what Aldo did and you do deserve to have your life and business back. I have no desire to stand in your way. If that means getting married, then let's do it.'

He tensed visibly and inwardly Angelica breathed a sigh of relief. He had been bluffing. But then his demeanor changed and he took her arm and led her over to where the men were standing outside the church building.

'Let's get going.'

Angelica's blood went cold. She resisted Leo's attempt to urge her into the dark interior of the chapel. 'No, wait.'

The other men had gone in ahead of them. Leo looked down at her. For a second, Angelica felt dizzy. Was she really standing here with Aldo just buried, still in her funeral clothes, and with Leo expecting her to walk down an aisle? In spite of how he'd rejected her before, she couldn't deny that she'd still had dreams... She shook her head to dislodge the humiliating reminder of the pull he'd had over her.

'Wait...'

He arched a dark brow. 'You thought I didn't mean it? Don't you remember that I don't bluff?'

A memory flashed back of this man taking off his shoes and socks by the Trevi fountain in central Rome, with Angelica looking on in horror saying, 'You wouldn't dare...' only to watch as he'd calmly rolled up his trousers to his knees and climbed over the fence around the fountain and stepped down into the blue/green water, beneath which shimmered all the coins thrown in by tourists making their wishes.

A cheer had gone up and he'd smiled at her and turned around, arms in the air, a moment that had gone viral. She couldn't even remember what they'd been talking about but clearly he'd called her bluff. He'd had to pay a fine for that act but the authorities had let him off any other charges, as charmed by him as she had been...

So, no, he didn't bluff. He obviously meant to go through with this outrageous act. And suddenly Angelica was somewhere between past and present, her body humming to be close to this man again, humming in a way that told her she hadn't got over him at all. *Physically,* she told herself desperately. Emotionally, he could never hurt her again.

She pulled her arm free of his loose grip. 'Are you kidnapping me all the way to the altar, Leo?'

He took a step back. 'You're free to go. But I can assure you that marrying me will be so much easier and efficient in the long term.'

'Because if I don't you'll drag me through the courts to get what's yours?'

'Something like that. Even if you were to sign over Aldo's shares to me, it wouldn't be that simple. It's your inheritance from him and it's bound up by all those legalities. Probate et cetera. But through marrying me, it will become my property too.'

She frowned. 'Won't probate still take time?'

He said, 'Yes, but marriage to you will expedite the process, helped by the fact that I've been proved innocent and have a right back to my company. It was your choice to marry Aldo, and to collude with him and to let me rot in jail. Now you face the consequences.'

Angelica's brain was racing. Leo had a point but he didn't know the truth of it. She'd had no choice. She couldn't tell Leo about the blackmail without revealing the truth about her family, and she couldn't trust what he would do with that information. He'd probably use it as Aldo had, to make her comply. She couldn't go through that again. They were safe now and she wasn't going to jeopardise their safety.

He'd also just assured her that if she walked away, he'd come after her and he'd end up finding out about them anyway.

'How long?' she blurted out.

'How long what?'

'How long would you want to be married?' She wasn't going to even contemplate this without a get-out date.

'Six months minimum.'

'One month.'

He shook his head. 'Not long enough.'

'Two months.'

He cocked his head on one side. 'Four months. That's about enough time to work out the legalities and establish myself on the scene.'

'Three months. That's the most I'll agree to.' Three months she could do. There was an end in sight. It wasn't insurmountable. And then she'd be free of this debt owed to Leo and she could *finally* move on with her life.

'OK.'

She blinked. 'OK?'

'Yes. But we get married right now and you're mine for the next three months.'

Angelica shivered delicately. He'd said those words, *you're mine*, to her before, sounding desperate. It was why she'd hoped that when she told him she loved him, he would feel the same. Surely he'd had to have felt it too…the intensity between them.

But he hadn't. And now she was in a bind with the man who had crushed her heart to pieces. But that was OK because she had no illusions any more. She was as cynical as he was. Probably even more.

'I will marry you, Leo, but I belong to no one, not

now, not ever. I also have work commitments that I'm not prepared to renege on. I have a professional reputation to consider.' She wasn't going to tell him about her jadedness with her job, and how she wanted to move on and do something more meaningful with her life.

'As long as you're available when I need you we won't have a problem. If there are conflicting interests we'll discuss it.'

How could he sound so reasonable when he'd just kidnapped her from her husband's funeral and was now about to march her down the aisle? Because he had been reasonable once. Kind, even. Part of what had made her fall in love with him was how he'd treated others and how he'd always had an air of being able to handle anything.

Any veneer of civility was well and truly gone though, and in that moment she said with feeling, 'I truly wish we'd never met.'

His jaw tightened and then he said, 'Too late for regrets.'

'You'll wish you never married me. Do you really think I'll make this easy for you?' She'd locked herself away mentally and emotionally from Aldo and she would utilise those skills again. Three months. She could do it.

He huffed an unamused laugh as he took her arm again. 'Believe me, after what I've been through, marriage to you will be a cakewalk. Time to start paying your dues, *cara*.'

He urged her in through the door into the gloomy

interior and when her eyes adjusted to the light, Angelica could see the men waiting for them near the altar. There was a priest, presumably to bless this non-wedding of a wedding. It was a farce, and yet, as Leo walked her down the aisle, it galled her to acknowledge that anger at the fact that her life was being derailed *again* wasn't her uppermost emotion, it was a mixture of far more conflicting things that she'd never expected to be feeling again.

And actually, it was fear she was feeling, fear that she might forget just how badly this man had hurt her, because seeing him again was reviving far too much and she was fast being hurtled into a future she'd never expected before she had time to catch up with herself. Or, worse, protect herself.

The hum of the aeroplane was the only sound. They were on their way to New York where Leo had a life and business to reclaim, with the help of his new wife. Angelica hadn't reacted when she'd been told of their destination.

Why didn't he feel more triumphant? Leo brooded as he sat in a sprawl across the aisle from his new wife. He'd achieved exactly what he'd set out to achieve. A swift and comprehensive lesson delivered to the woman who had betrayed him with her lover/husband, *his* ex-business partner. But instead of triumph all he felt was a certain level of frustration.

She'd barely looked at him during the short and businesslike marriage ceremony. The most emotion she'd shown had been when they'd had to exchange rings and Leo had held up a gold band only for her to lift her hand where Aldo's ring had still sat. She'd said, 'I already have one. It seems a waste to use another one.'

A red tide of emotion had made Leo bite out, 'Take it off.'

She'd just looked at him, face pale and set. Eventually she'd removed it and handed it to him, and he'd slipped the ring he'd bought onto her finger, very aware of the distaste deep inside him in that moment for what he was doing and yet he couldn't *not*.

The urge to cleave her to him even like this was too strong. He told himself he welcomed her hatred and resentment. Her reluctance. The more she hated this whole situation, the more it would salve his bruised soul. But…it *wasn't*.

She was sitting on the cream leather couch opposite him, shoes off, legs pulled up and to the side. Hair down and over her shoulders, in waves of dark brown silk. She was on her phone, intensely absorbed, fingers moving fast as she communicated with someone.

An unsavoury thought occurred to him. 'Do you have a lover?'

She looked up and those unusual green eyes caught him right in the gut, much as they had when he'd first seen her.

'That's none of your business.'

His insides tightened at the thought that she was communicating with someone. 'I won't tolerate infidelity.'

She put her phone down on the seat beside her. Face

down, Leo noticed. He had to curb the urge to reach across and pick it up. He'd never been jealous over a woman. *Until this one.*

She sighed. 'No, I don't have a lover.'

Leo didn't believe her. He knew who she was now. A liar and a cheat.

'Do you?' She looked at him.

Leo felt like laughing, but didn't. He shook his head. 'No, I don't.'

A slightly panicked expression crossed her face. 'We aren't sharing a bed.'

Leo's blood spiked as if rejecting that assertion, every cell humming with awareness, his body telling him that as much as he wanted to deny it, he still wanted her. But he said, 'Don't worry, I have no intention of sleeping with Aldo's leftovers. This will be purely an exercise in appearances.'

Everything within Angelica demanded that she defend herself against Leo's low opinion—*leftovers*—but she bit her tongue. He had no right to know the truth of her existence. He'd got her where he wanted her for the next three months and then she would walk away.

She told herself it was a good thing that he no longer wanted her. *You still want him.* Even now her skin felt sensitive and the blood too close to the surface. She couldn't stop her gaze from getting caught on his jaw, his shoulders, his chest and down...that lean waist, those formidable thighs.

She resolutely fixed her gaze on his face, not that that was any better. She'd traced those hard-cut planes with her fingers and mouth too many times to count.

'Good,' she bit out. 'We're on the same page.'

Appearances. She could do appearances. After all, she was a model, it was her job to *appear* and put a mask on. She would just approach this as a three-month gig. Something audacious occurred to her and for the first time since she'd seen Leo again she felt a smidgeon of control. He might have compelled her to be his wife but he couldn't control any other aspect of her. She certainly didn't have to give him an easy ride.

'What is that look?'

Angelica felt a jolt in her gut. She'd forgotten how easily he could read her. And she'd spent the last three years hiding behind a serene mask. She couldn't let it drop now. She thought of something to divert his attention, 'Actually…if you're so concerned with appearances, won't it attract the wrong sort of attention when people realise you've married the widow of your ex-partner, the man who put you in jail?'

He shrugged. 'It's not ideal, no, but in the circumstances I don't think I could have found a more convenient wife. It's common knowledge we were together before. People will just assume you're the fickle one, following whoever has the money. I'm sure something or someone else will come along to divert their attention away from speculation.'

At that moment Angelica vowed to do everything in her power to ensure that people's attention wasn't diverted. And if it helped to hurry up the demise of this marriage, then all the better.

She forced a sweet smile, 'I'm sure you're right.'

Leo finally looked away from her face and down

at the tablet in his hand. Angelica sucked in a breath. He still affected her. After three years encasing herself in ice, it was disconcerting to *feel* things again. Even if it was just physical sensations. Not emotional, just physical.

Her phone buzzed silently on the seat beside her and she turned it over to see a message from her mother with a sad crying-face emoji. Her heart felt sore. She'd told them she wouldn't be able to see them just yet, but, for her, knowing that they were safe and getting on with their lives was enough to sustain her. It had to be, because she had nothing else.

As if hearing her thoughts, Leo asked abruptly, 'Why do you have no luggage?'

She looked at him again as she pulled her legs out from under her. They were getting crampy. She saw how his gaze dropped to her thighs before coming back up. The slight flare of colour in his cheeks. Maybe he wasn't as immune to Aldo's *leftovers* as he made out to be. Damn it but that shouldn't be making her feel a spurt of adrenalin. Her heart rate increasing. Blood flowing to parts of her body that had lain dormant since...*him*. She pushed that uncomfortable revelation to one side.

'Because there was nothing I wanted to take with me.' It was true. She'd wanted nothing of what her husband had bought her. He'd had all of her own personal items taken and destroyed.

A swooping sense of panic gripped her as she realised that she had kept one personal item. A necklace that Leo had given her when they'd been together. Not an expensive item...but sentimental.

She could feel it almost burning against the skin of her upper chest now like a brand. She sent up silent thanks she was wearing a high-neck dress so he couldn't see it. She'd put it on, almost without thinking, as soon as she'd heard the news that Aldo was dead.

Not that Leo would remember the moment when they'd been walking hand in hand along a small Venetian street and they'd passed by a tourist shop full of Murano glass trinkets. One had caught her eye, a heart-shaped piece of glass on a gold chain. Green and gold and orange. Like a beating heart.

Leo had stopped and seen where her gaze had fallen and as soon as she'd realised she'd blushed and tried to pull away but before she'd known what was happening, he'd been urging her into the shop and had asked the proprietor to take the necklace out of the window before paying for it.

Angelica had objected but secretly she'd been touched. Her father had never exhibited such thoughtful gestures to her mother. Leo had tied the necklace around her neck and it had been the following day that Angelica had told him she loved him, high in a beautiful frescoed room in his apartment in a palazzo on the Grand Canal.

She'd never considered herself a sentimental person, given to romantic whims, and yet she'd fallen hard for this man and she'd taken out her heart and presented him with it.

Only for him to crush it.

And then when Aldo had put her in an impossible situation, he'd only hammered home the realisation that she'd been beyond weak and naive. Never again.

Leo cut through the unwelcome memories, 'When we get to New York, I'll arrange for someone to meet with you and you can give them a list of whatever you need. I'll also arrange for a stylist to come and discuss what you'll need for social events.'

'I have my own money and I know how to dress myself,' Angelica pointed out.

'While you're married to me you won't spend your own money.'

Another reminder, as if Angelica needed it, that Leo had always been incredibly generous. The opposite to Aldo, who'd been mean and tight. The only reason he hadn't got his hands on her earnings was because she'd questioned why he would need them, wasn't he rich enough? His colossal pride had stopped him from pursuing her money ever again. So at least she'd had that—her financial independence.

It chafed to have a man pay for her but Angelica told herself now that Leo owed her as much as she owed him—if she'd never met him she wouldn't have been humiliated and she wouldn't have met his business partner—so she just shrugged minutely and said carelessly, 'Whatever.'

She picked up a magazine from a pile on the coffee table near the seat and idly flicked through it, no more interested in the glossy photos than the fact that it was *her* face staring out at her in many of the pictures.

She willed the plane to get to New York as soon as possible because the sooner they got on with this charade, the sooner it would be over and she could finally reunite with her family.

CHAPTER THREE

'I NEVER ASKED you where you were planning on going after the funeral.'

Angelica didn't turn around from the window where she was looking out at the view, which spanned from where they were in midtown Manhattan, all the way down to the One World Trade Center.

The Hudson River sparkled under the low autumnal sun. Flashes of gold and brown were visible here and there.

She didn't respond to Leo's remark, saying, 'I assumed you'd be going to the apartment on the Upper East Side.' It was where she'd spent a lot of time over the last three years and if Aldo said he was coming to New York she'd invariably find a reason to leave before he arrived.

'I believe Aldo had it redecorated.'

Angelica shuddered delicately. He had, and it hadn't been good. 'You could say that.'

Leo's tone was dry. 'I can imagine exactly how he did it. Lots of gold and bling. It'll be up for sale as soon as I can get it back into my name and on the market.'

Angelica glanced at him where he'd come to stand

beside her at the window. This apartment was in a futuristically designed building, gleaming and soaring into the sky. She found she liked it better than the slightly stuffy atmosphere around Central Park. Even though she loved that park.

Curious, she asked, 'How can you afford this now…? Isn't everything still tied up in the company in Aldo's name?'

He looked at her. 'Your name.'

A reminder of her worth to him now. 'Believe me, the sooner I can disentangle myself from what you rightfully own, the better.'

'I'll believe that when you have a piece of paper in front of you with your signature on it. You did warn me you wouldn't make this easy.'

Yes, she had, but she hadn't meant it like that. Angelica turned towards him, feeling injured, 'You know I was never interested in anything like that.'

He raised a brow. 'Do I? After you ran straight from me into Aldo's bed?'

Angelica stifled her response. How could she deny how it looked? It killed her that she couldn't just blurt out the truth but she daredn't. There was too much at stake. Her mother and brother. Awful things had happened to family members of people who'd ever had the misfortune of getting entangled with the Mafia in Sicily. They were safe now but that could all change if Leo chose to use them as leverage as Aldo had.

The only reason she'd been relatively safe was because she'd got out early and had become an internationally recognisable face. They didn't need the kind of PR that would come from harming someone like her. But her mother and brother were still at some level of risk. As Aldo had proven only too effectively.

Leo continued, 'My personal wealth and assets were frozen while I was in prison, which inadvertently helped me because all Aldo had access to was the business finances and any assets in the company name. Something to be grateful for. Needless to say I won't be going into business with anyone else, ever again.'

'Not everyone is Aldo,' Angelica pointed out.

'I don't care, I won't take that risk.'

'You knew him since you were kids, how did you not see that he was harbouring such resentment against you?'

Leo had told her of how, when he'd gone to the mainland to an orphanage run by a charity that specifically helped to remove children from the tentacles of Mafia gangs, he'd bonded with Aldo, who'd also come there in similar circumstances.

Leo looked away, out of the window. 'It was the biggest mistake of my life, trusting that man.'

'You loved him. He was like a brother.'

Leo looked at her again and she could see the bleakness in his expression. 'My brothers were killed in front of me. Aldo was a leech who played the long game.'

Again Angelica had to curb her tongue. She'd heard Aldo drunkenly rant over and over again about how he and Leo had been equal until it had become clear that Leo was on a level that Aldo could never hope to achieve. Jealousy and bitterness had eaten away at him until he'd masterminded Leo's downfall, which had ultimately led to Aldo's downfall too.

'You haven't answered me—where were you going after the funeral?'

Angelica said as carelessly as she could, 'Spain.'

'Why Spain?'

To reunite with her family. She shrugged one shoulder. 'I'd booked a holiday for myself.'

He made a whistling sound. 'Straight after your husband's funeral? With no luggage? I don't think so.'

Angelica looked at Leo and his eyes were dark, bottomless. He said, 'Whoever your lover is, you cut off all contact now, understand? He'll have you back soon enough, if he wants to wait around.'

She shouldn't be surprised that he didn't believe that she was telling the truth on the plane. The thought of a lover was laughable. It had taken all of her energy to deal with a petulant, immature, vengeful husband and try to keep her professional life afloat.

'Believe what you want, Leo, I'm not going to waste my breath again.'

She was suddenly overcome with a wave of weariness. It had been a tumultuous day and she still wasn't entirely sure if she was dreaming. 'If you don't mind, I'd like to get out of these clothes and wash and rest. It's been a long day.'

Leo felt a trickle of discomfort when he had to acknowledge the air of fragility around Angelica that he'd noticed earlier, compounded now by shadows under her eyes.

He still couldn't quite believe she was here, in front of him, wearing his ring. *And still wearing the clothes she'd buried her husband in.* Suddenly he wanted any association with Aldo Bianchi gone.

'Fine, absolutely, make yourself at home.'

A glint of something like humour came into her eye. 'Why, thank you, so considerate.'

It mocked Leo for letting his guard drop for a moment. This woman wasn't fragile, she was just human. Aldo had died of an overdose, Leo had to assume that Angelica had partaken of that lifestyle too, even though when he'd known her, she'd been vehemently against drugs, and hadn't even drunk that much.

She was turning away from him to leave the room but he caught her arm in his hand, relishing the feel of her toned muscles. She looked up at him and he could see how she held herself tightly. Tense. Which automatically made him want to move that hand from her arm to her waist, and put his other hand there and pull her into him until he could feel those womanly curves pressed against his body.

Angry with his wayward libido, he said more harshly than he intended, 'If you've changed your habits to include taking recreational drugs like your husband, I won't tolerate it.'

A flash of disgust came over her face before it was gone. She pulled her arm free and said with a mocking smile, 'What a shame. If I'd known a coke habit would turn you off the marriage, I would have mentioned it a lot sooner.'

But then her smile faded and she was deadly serious. 'I've never done drugs and I still don't do drugs.'

She turned and walked out of the room, back straight, legs long. Hair like silk down her back. Regal, stunning.

Leo turned to face the view, tugging at his tie, staring out unseeingly. Once again he questioned his sanity but then he told himself again that he never would have found a woman willing to be his convenient wife with no strings attached. And Angelica owed him. Even she acknowledged that.

But the reality of following through on his plans, the reality of looking at her, smelling her scent, talking to her—convenience was the last thing on his mind. It was a tangle of emotions and desires and the anger that had kept him going for the last three years. He smiled mirthlessly. Yes, his anger at, and hatred for, Angelica Malgeri had actually helped him survive the last three years, because he'd pictured this very scenario. Having her at his mercy. Aldo too, but Aldo had not afforded him that opportunity.

He cursed his introspection. He had to stop ruminating on the past and get on with rebuilding his future. With his new wife at his side.

Even though Angelica was exhausted, she couldn't rest. She'd found what she assumed to be a guest suite, decorated in muted elegant tones with a luxurious cream carpet. She'd taken off the funeral clothes and had a blissful shower, scrubbing every bit of the last three years from her body. And now she was in a robe with her hair piled up turban-style on her head. She'd come out onto the small terrace outside the bedroom and was taking in the view as dusk stole over the iconic skyline of Manhattan.

In spite of everything that had happened and the fact that within hours of burying her husband she was now married to her ex-lover, she couldn't deny that she felt a measure of peace. The kind of peace that had been elusive for three years. *Since Leo rejected you.*

Even though she knew she couldn't trust Leo, she knew he wouldn't hurt her. Life with Aldo and his moods and mercurial nature had kept her in a constant adrenalised state. At least she'd been able to use her work as an excuse to stay away from him as much as possible and he'd never really objected because his ego had loved having a supermodel for a wife. They were only seen together for public events, and as few of those as Angelica could get away with.

She'd had to fly back at short notice on a private jet from Bangkok to Rome in order to placate him when he'd had a tantrum that she wouldn't be with him for an event. But thankfully those incidents hadn't been too common. Aldo had never mentioned specifically what he'd do if he went after her mother and brother, the threat of any kind of harm to them had been enough. She'd never been able to push things too far.

But at least with Leo, it would just be about getting through the charade of the next three months, less if she could manage it. She was counting on being able to encourage Leo to change his mind about this marriage. After being Aldo's wife, and after fake smiling her way through social engagement after social engagement, doing everything not to stand out, she now knew exactly what to do, to stand out.

The following morning Angelica woke up and it took her a couple of minutes to figure out where she was. On another continent. Married to a different man. Her ex-lover. *Leo.* She sat up in bed. She was still wearing the robe she'd put on after the shower.

She couldn't hear any sounds and, after freshening up, she belted the robe tighter around her—because it was either that or what she'd been wearing yesterday—and went out into the apartment.

All was quiet and then she heard noises from the kitchen area. She went to investigate and found an older man dressed in smart black trousers and a black top. He smiled and introduced himself as Michael. 'I'm Mr Falzone's apartment manager. He told me to let you know that he's gone to meetings but he's arranged for the glam squad to come at four to help you get ready.'

Ready for what? Angelica didn't ask. 'I... OK.' Obviously there was an event this evening and Leo expected her to go with him.

'What would you like for brunch?'

She gulped. 'What time is it?'

'Midday.'

She'd slept for hours. 'I'm so sorry, I didn't realise.' Michael waved a hand, 'Mr Falzone said you weren't to be disturbed. I can prepare something for you now?'

Angelica wanted to get out onto the streets and breathe some fresh air and orientate herself but— 'I'd like to go out actually, but I have a small problem, I didn't bring any luggage with me and I only have what I was wearing while travelling.'

Michael walked out of the kitchen and said, 'Come with me.'

Bemused, Angelica followed him to a room adjacent to her bedroom suite. He opened a door and she looked inside. It was a dressing room, full of clothes. She walked in. They were all in her size. An array of casual clothes and evening-wear. Sports clothes. Underwear. She turned to Michael. 'How long has this been here?'

'Mr Falzone had a stylist deliver the clothes this morning. I have her number if you need to contact her for anything but she'll be back later with the glam squad.'

The fact that this hadn't already been here before her arrival settled something inside Angelica. Leo obviously hadn't taken it for granted that she would comply.

A flash of gold caught her eye and she reached out and touched a dress. It was like a liquid waterfall of silken folds. She recognised the iconic designer label.

'If there's anything else?'

Angelica forced a smile at the man. 'No, thank you, this is very helpful.'

He left and Angelica pulled out some jeans and a

long-sleeved top. Fresh underwear. It didn't surprise her that Leo had done this, although the speed with which he'd managed to do it was impressive, but he'd always been generous when they'd been together before.

She found a soft, light leather jacket and grabbed her bag and left the apartment, taking the elevator all the way down to the ground floor and then stepping outside.

The air was cool, but hadn't yet got to that frigidly cold state. It reminded her of a snowbound Christmas she'd spent here. She'd actually been happy to be here alone because Aldo had been in Europe and the adverse weather had meant she couldn't travel. He hadn't been happy of course because there had been several high-profile winter social events to attend, but there hadn't been much he could do about it.

Angelica had called her mother and brother and they'd video called for hours. She hadn't revealed the extent of the threat she, or they, were under, not wanting them to worry. She'd had to let them believe that she was still under advice to avoid physical contact in order to shore up their safety. She'd also used work as an excuse. She'd despised Aldo for that, because it would have been safe enough after a year of no contact to visit them. But he'd ruined that chance.

And, thanks to Leo, she was still being held back from seeing them, but now at least she knew they were safe. And she might not be free, yet, but she was a lot freer than she had been.

She sucked in a deep breath of Manhattan's finest

air and went to find a diner. Clinging onto her independence as much as possible had helped her survive marriage to Aldo, and she was sure it would do the same with Leo.

Except, you don't mind spending time with him, pointed out a small voice. Angelica scowled and slipped a pair of shades on against the late autumn sun. She'd merely lost one gaoler, who had been replaced by another. Leo Falzone meant nothing to her and any notion that he still affected her was just down to shock and memories.

It was early evening and the stylist and glam squad had left the apartment. Angelica hadn't seen Leo all day but he had returned to the apartment and there was a knock on the dressing-room door now. Her silly heart kicked up a notch. 'Yes?'

'We'll be leaving in five minutes.'

Angelica felt like childishly sticking her tongue out at the door but refrained and said, 'OK.' He hadn't checked in with her all day, had merely married her, brought her across the globe, dumped her at his apartment and now expected her to perform like a puppet on a string for his benefit.

Not so different from Aldo after all. She checked her reflection in the mirror. She looked the epitome of classic elegance. Hair up in a smooth chignon. A strapless black sheath of a dress. High heels. Discreet jewellery. Understated make-up.

Aldo would have approved. And she was sure that Leo would take one look, and also approve. Something about that now chafed. She could walk out of the door now, a picture of acceptable perfection. She *could*. But she wouldn't.

With an efficiency born of changing clothes a million times a day for work, Angelica took off the dress and hung it back up before choosing an entirely different outfit.

Leo paced back and forth in the main living area. He was wearing a classic black tuxedo and he'd never noticed before that it felt constrictive, but it did, around his neck.

He'd found it hard to concentrate today, distracted by Angelica. Even when he wasn't with her. He knew she'd left the apartment and for a couple of hours, until he'd been notified of her return, he hadn't been entirely sure she wouldn't just disappear. As much as an internationally renowned model could disappear.

She'd always been independent. It was something he'd forgotten about her. It was one of the qualities that had attracted him to her. She'd been so much more grounded and self-sufficient than other women he'd met.

But he'd also felt uncomfortable about just leaving her at the apartment, and he'd intended calling to let her know about the event tonight but the meeting with his legal team to get the process under way of putting the business back in his name had been intricate and intense.

But things were under way and soon Leo would have everything back in his name. Never again would he be caught out and now, with his wife by his side, there was no reason why— There was a sound from behind him and he turned around to see Angelica in the doorway.

He frowned. She was wearing jeans that clung like a second skin to every inch of her long legs and shapely hips, and a plain black T-shirt. High heels. Her hair was up though, in a smooth and elegant chignon. She wore chunky diamond jewellery around her neck and wrist.

He said, 'You're not ready.'

'I am ready. I didn't feel especially like wearing a dress.'

'It's a black-tie event.'

She indicated the T-shirt. 'I'm wearing black.'

Leo assessed the situation in an instant. So this was how she was going to play it. Something kicked to life inside him, a spurt of excitement, even though he wanted to deny it. He walked towards her and saw her eyes widen, a little flush come into her cheeks. He stopped just in front of her. 'You know I don't respond to bluffs, Angel.'

There was a spark in her eyes at *Angel*. She tipped up her chin. *Dio*. She was stunning. And treacherous. He couldn't afford to forget that. And three years with Aldo had clearly encouraged a penchant for games.

She said, 'I'm not bluffing, *Leo*.'

He hid his reaction to *Leo*. 'Ready to go, then?'

He saw the chink of uncertainty and then it was gone. 'Ready.'

He put his hand lightly around her arm, the touch

of skin on skin igniting his blood. He gritted his jaw against her effect. She was a siren and he'd chosen to marry her so he would just have to control himself.

They were almost at the door when she stopped in front of the mirror to check herself. He let her arm go. She said, 'Coco Chanel's advice was to always remove one thing before you walked out the door.'

Leo said, 'I can help with that.' From her head, he plucked the diamanté comb holding her chignon in place. Her hair fell down under its own weight, tumbling around her shoulders in silken waves.

He had to curb the urge to bury his hands in her hair and left the comb on the table. 'There, perfect. Let's go.'

There was some sense of satisfaction in the surprised expression on her face but by the time they stepped outside and into the back of the car, her face was a cool mask again.

In the car, Leo was acutely aware of Angelica's long legs provocatively encased in that soft denim. The T-shirt that did little to hide the swell of her perfect breasts.

But it wasn't just her physical perfection that had first caught his eye, it had been something in her manner. Unguarded. Genuine. At odds with the people around them at the exclusive event in Rome.

They'd bumped into each other when he'd been jostled by someone moving through the crowd. She'd ended up with a glass of champagne down the front of her pristine pale-pink evening gown. Leo had braced himself for an explosion of feminine outrage but she'd looked up at him and smiled and he'd almost collapsed under the impact of her beauty. Thick brown hair, caught up and exposing a long neck, high cheekbones and defined jaw. The greenest eyes he'd ever seen, under black brows. Long lashes. And her mouth, wide and generous.

She'd smiled and held up the empty glass, saying, 'Thank you, I was just looking for a reason to give my excuses to leave.'

Leo had shaken his head, trying to get out something coherent, an apology for knocking her drink, but she'd already been moving backwards, away, and instead of apologising he'd croaked out, 'Who are you?' Even though he'd realised that there *was* something familiar about her.

She'd answered, 'I'm no one. Thanks again.' And she'd turned and left, slipping through the crowd and disappearing so quickly that he'd wondered if he'd just dreamt up that little exchange with the most beautiful woman he'd ever seen.

The next day Leo had seen her face high on a billboard advertising a very luxe brand of jewellery. *I'm no one.* She was 'Angelica', one of the few models whose first name was enough to identify them. He hadn't stopped until he'd contacted her and until she'd agreed to meet him for a date.

In the years since then, he'd wondered if that first *meeting* had been as innocently spontaneous as it had seemed. Had she in fact contrived to bump into him and pique his interest? Only to then run into the arms of his business partner once he'd told her he wouldn't commit?

It was a theory he'd found himself clinging to because it was easier to believe that, and that she'd been playing him from the very first moment they'd met, than to live with the fact that she'd been as innocent as he'd believed her to be. And that he'd let a woman get too close, after years of keeping them at a distance for fear of an emotional connection that could lead to loss and pain.

She'd captivated him and that was a weakness he'd never forgive himself for. But he'd learnt his lesson. Now he was in control. She wouldn't play him again.

A car horn sounded nearby in the traffic jerking Leo back into the present moment.

He felt something in his pocket and he remembered. He took a box out and said, 'Actually, I'm afraid we're going to have to add something again.'

She looked at him and then down at the small velvet box. He opened it and her eyes widened fractionally.

Angelica looked at what was obviously meant to be an engagement ring. And it caught her right in the gut. Because she would have chosen it for herself. It was a square emerald stone, flanked by two smaller sapphires, in a platinum setting.

A vast contrast to the ostentatious and totally over-the-top massive pear-drop diamond that Aldo had made her wear. She'd had to remember to put it on when around him. After he'd died she'd gone straight out and found the nearest homeless shelter and had handed it over as a donation, telling them they could do what they liked with it.

But this was...lovely. Before she could stop him, Leo was taking it out of the box and reaching for her hand, sliding it onto her finger where the wedding band sat.

She looked at him and said almost accusingly, 'It fits.'

He drawled, 'The perks of having a wife who is one of the most well-known models in the world. Your sizes are a matter of public information.'

Angelica pulled her hand away and made a choked sound and looked out of the window. He'd just articulated another reason why she wanted to leave the industry—the fact that she was a public commodity. A public clothes horse. Yet, she felt churlish because the business had been very good to her and it had saved her sanity when married to Aldo. She did appreciate it but she was ready to move on. She wasn't even sure where to exactly, but she knew she hungered for something more meaningful.

The car pulled to a smooth stop outside one of Manhattan's most iconic buildings, wide steps leading up to a massive entrance garlanded with foliage and flaming lanterns. The steps were covered in a red carpet and thronged with people in a glittering array of colours, and with jewellery sparkling at ears, throats, wrists and fingers.

Leo got out of the car and came around to help Angelica out. When she would have pulled her hand back, he held it. She looked up at him. They were at the bottom of the steps and he lifted her hand and pressed a kiss to her palm. It was unexpected and felt shockingly intimate. An arrow of pure lust shot straight to the core of her body.

He was urging her with him, up the steps before she had time to absorb all the sensations of that one relatively chaste touch. She wanted to pull her hand away but the bank of paparazzi on one side had already noticed her and were calling out her name, and Leo's. Acting on autopilot, she stopped and posed for the photographers, Leo by her side.

Voices rang out, *'Angelica, over here, please! Who are you wearing? Are you and Falzone really married?'*

She ignored the questions and forced a smile. They moved up the steps and got closer to the door. By the time they had reached the entrance, Angelica realised she was holding onto Leo's hand for support as much as to put forward a display of unity. Paparazzi had never bothered her too much before but now she felt exposed. Self-conscious. Even more so when they stepped into the magnificent ballroom space and Angelica knew she stood out like a sore thumb in her jeans and T-shirt, even if they were designer label.

She tried not to let the prickle of regret or her conscience bother her. After all, she was trying to encourage Leo to realise that marrying her had been a mistake. But, as they entered the room and moved through the crowd, her choice of attire seemed to be making waves but for all the wrong reasons. When Leo was accosted by someone, the other man's partner said to Angelica, 'You're making the rest of us look overdressed and fussy.'

Angelica smiled weakly, 'That really wasn't my intention.' She'd just wanted to irritate Leo.

The woman winked at her, 'Believe me, if I thought I could get away with jeans and a T-shirt I'd be joining you. These dress codes are so outdated.'

The couple moved away and Leo bent his head towards Angelica saying with a definite hint of humour in his voice, 'It looks like your stunt isn't going as well as you planned it.'

Angelica smiled sweetly and looked up at Leo, trying not to be distracted by the growth of stubble along his jaw, stubble he hadn't attempted to shave away to look more...presentable. 'Oh, believe me, I could engineer any number of situations to draw adverse attention.' She snagged a glass of champagne from a passing waiter's tray and took a healthy sip, and said, 'I never was good at holding my drink.'

Leo neatly took the glass out of Angelica's hand and placed it on another passing waiter's tray. 'Don't even think about it. Let's have a dance, *darling*. After all, our wedding was so rushed we didn't have time for the festivities.'

Angelica scowled at Leo. 'Hardly my fault.' But he was already tucking her hand into his and bringing her with him through the crowd to where people had started to dance in front of a band playing smooth tunes.

He pulled her close to his body and Angelica tensed against the inevitable way she wanted to cleave to him.

She suddenly appreciated that at least while married to Aldo, she hadn't had to battle her own rogue hormones. She'd been quite happy to let him pursue his extra-marital affairs with women. And men.

Leo noted, 'You've lost weight.'

Angelica tensed. The result of living on her nerves for the last few years. 'Not really your business.'

'I'm your husband.'

Angelica snorted softly. 'And as such you care for my welfare?'

Leo tipped up her chin with his finger. She had no choice but to look at him. 'As my wife, of course I care about your welfare.'

Her heart twisted. She'd once thought that he really had cared about her welfare. And he had. In bed. Not out of it. Not long-term. After all, through her association with him, he'd practically handed Aldo the invitation to use her for his nefarious ends. The fact that he'd also tried to ruin Leo wasn't much comfort.

'If I'm too thin for you—'

He pulled her closer and another couple swept past. 'I didn't say that.'

Angelica felt spiky and exposed. Defensive. Leo's chest rumbled against hers when he spoke. 'You don't need me to tell you that you're easily the most beautiful woman here.'

She wanted to duck her head. She knew that she was lucky to have been blessed with a face and body that photographed well, but she knew that there was so much more to her and at one time, she thought Leo had seen it too.

'I've been working hard the last few years.'

As they spoke, Angelica was aware that Leo was effortlessly moving them around the floor. She didn't even have to think, he was so easy to follow.

'Are you saying you didn't want to spend time with your beloved husband?'

Angelica's skin prickled. He was very close to the bone there. And she felt tired of keeping up a facade. 'My marriage with Aldo wasn't exactly…all that it seemed.'

Leo tugged her closer again to avoid another couple. Angelica's breasts were crushed to his chest and her nipples drew into hard points, helplessly reacting to his proximity. She was drowning in his scent.

'Are you saying you made a mistake?'

Angelica felt like laughing out loud but stifled it. 'I'm just saying that things weren't perfect.'

Leo's tone was dry. 'You're hardly the picture of a widow in grief so I think that's the most honest thing you've said since we met again.'

And then, 'Why did you do it? What was Aldo offering you? What did you want?'

Angelica stopped as the song came to an end and pulled back in Leo's arms. How did she begin to frame an answer to that without putting her family in danger again?

She said, 'You lost the right to know anything about me when you told me to leave, three years ago.' She pulled free completely and walked off the dance floor.

CHAPTER FOUR

Leo watched Angelica weave through the crowd, and noticed how everyone she passed turned to look at her. He could commiserate. She was captivating. He also noticed, now that he was alone, a creeping sense of claustrophobia as people brushed past him, making a faint sense of nausea swirl in his gut.

He'd noticed this since leaving prison, the way he was acutely aware of crowds and quickly felt a need to move, find space. He'd spent three years in cramped conditions, fighting for his own space. It was only natural. But it was only now that he realised that Angelica had successfully distracted him enough to not be aware of it here.

But now he was. He gritted his jaw and focused on her again to drive out the rising sense of panic, plunging after her into the crowd. Mercifully the crowd thinned out and Leo was free again. He saw Angelica at the entrance, her back to him.

He could still feel the fragility in her body, held against him, reinforcing his impression of vulnerability. He shook his head. An erroneous impression.

As was the notion that her marriage to Aldo was

a regret. She'd amassed a fortune through her marriage to that man—Leo's fortune—and he didn't expect for one second that she was going to just sign away her rights to it.

But, the following day in a sleek office high above Manhattan, Leo watched Angelica do exactly that. Every piece of paper that was put in front of her with an asterix beside where she had to sign, she signed, without even looking at the rest of the document. She'd refused the offer of having her own legal representation present.

Leo watched her from a corner of the room. She was surrounded by legal assistants, unfazed, her dark hair shining, pulled over one shoulder carelessly, exposing her neck.

She was wearing a loose silk top and jeans. Flat shoes. The luxe/louche uniform of the top model. The papers were full of them today. A front-page splash. Breathless speculation about what it could possibly mean for Angelica to turn up at an event with her new husband...*in jeans*!

Nothing about the fact that she had been widowed and remarried within an indecently short amount of time. Nothing about Leo's bid to reclaim what was his. And, he was recognising now, that wasn't necessarily a bad thing. As much as he needed to rehabilitate his image, he didn't necessarily need the scrutiny on his business affairs, the speculation as to how Aldo could have wreaked so much havoc because, with Leo in jail and disgraced, he'd had full control of everything. That was a weakness Leo would never forgive himself for and he didn't want people speculating that it could happen again. *Which it wouldn't. Ever.* So perhaps it was not such a bad thing that Angelica was drawing attention, even if for her controversial sartorial choices.

One of the assistants looked up at Leo. 'All signed.'

Leo pushed off the window he'd been leaning against and walked over to the table where another assistant was gathering up the documents. His chief legal advisor said, 'The only other documents to sign are the ones in Rome.'

Ah, yes. The most important legal documents; they hadn't been ready to sign before they'd left Italy. The documents that related to the fact that it had been Leo who had set up the business. Aldo had tried to change history while in control, naming himself as the brainchild behind Falzone Industries, and changing its name. They would have to return to Rome for that, as Aldo's legal team was based there.

Perhaps Leo was being complacent in assuming Angelica's amenability here would be the same in Rome. Maybe that was her plan, to lull him into a false sense of security before hitting him with terms and conditions, which he had fully expected.

But now, she put down the pen and stood up, turning to face him. Nothing in her expression to indicate any nefarious plans. But then she'd always been good at projecting innocence.

'If you don't mind, I told a designer friend I'd do a photo shoot for her new collection while I'm in town.'

Leo felt slightly wrong-footed. She wasn't heading out to lunch. Or to go back and lounge in the apartment. Or going shopping. She was going to work.

'Of course. We have an event to attend this evening, leaving the apartment at six p.m.'

'I'll be back by then.'

'The driver will take you wherever you need to go and wait for you.'

'It's OK, they've arranged transport for me. It's waiting outside.'

Leo was reminded that she'd always valued her independence. Clearly Aldo hadn't changed that. Something about that heartened him even in the midst of her throwing up contradictions he didn't like to consider.

'See you back at the apartment.'

She nodded and left the office, appearing totally unconcerned that she'd just signed away her right to a majority share in Leo's business. But the real test would be in Rome when she signed the paperwork there because up until that point she could still cause major problems for Leo. So he wasn't taking anything for granted.

It was shortly after Angelica had left the office that they received word that the rest of the paperwork in Rome was now ready. Leo had his assistant cancel all upcoming plans so they could return to Rome as soon as possible.

Angelica felt that prickle of her conscience again later that evening as she regarded herself in the mirror. What she was wearing now would make what she'd worn the previous night look positively elegant and refined.

She refused to let nerves assail her. She'd already started the process of untangling herself from Aldo's toxic legacy today by signing away most of what she'd inherited over to Leo. She had no desire for anything that man had touched, or corrupted. Even if she didn't have her own money, she wouldn't take a cent. It wasn't hers.

The rest would happen in Rome—Leo had sent her a text today alerting her that they'd be travelling there the following day, to meet with Aldo's lawyers. He clearly didn't fully trust that she wasn't going to turn around at the eleventh hour tomorrow and lay down demands. He would soon see though. And hopefully that would then be enough to convince him to let her go. To end this farcical marriage. To let her get back to her life. And her family. Once she'd proved that she had no designs on anything of his.

But for now, all she could do was test Leo's patience again. She tweaked her hair, pulled back into a high ponytail, and stepped into sky-high bright red stilettos. She took a deep breath and went into the main living area where Leo was ready and waiting, in a tuxedo, this time with a white coat and bow tie. He looked so devastatingly gorgeous that it took a second for Angelica to notice that his face had gone red and his eyes were bugging out of his head.

Sounding choked, he said, 'What is that?'

'It's a dress.' Even Angelica winced at that. It *was*

technically a dress but she could appreciate that it might defy such a banal description.

Leo felt as if his eyeballs were burning. Certainly Angelica's image would be forever branded onto his brain. A dress, she'd said? He would have laughed if he'd been capable. But right now he was in the eye of a storm that gripped him on so many levels he couldn't think straight.

He had impressions. Red. Lace. Defying gravity. *Naked.* Outrageous. He tried to be rational, to formulate his thoughts. Piece together what he was looking at. He knew he wasn't exactly sartorially experimental, so maybe he was being too hasty.

The...*dress*...did obey some conventions. Material clung to Angelica's breasts—how? Leo didn't even want to know because it looked as if the lace was spray-painted onto those perfectly shaped orbs of flesh. He could see the thrust of her nipples and blood went straight to his groin.

There was a vee in the material that went to her midriff, then the see-through lace clung to her hips and thighs and stopped, around mid-thigh. There were sleeves on her arms, but not up as far as her shoulders. A small red flower was tied to her neck in a choker.

His gaze travelled down over her endless legs to where her feet were encased in red. Towering, spindly heels.

All in all, he could definitely say that the quota of flesh to material was vastly in favour of flesh. Bare flesh. Plump, succulent flesh. Honed. Olive-skinned.

Soft like satin. Because he could think of nothing else now except how she'd felt under his hands, soft and yielding and hot and moist and—

'You cannot wear that.' Mercifully he'd found his voice. Just in time. Before he went up in flames and disgraced himself.

'I promised my friend I'd wear it to help promote her work. She's just won Emerging Designer of the Year.'

'So evidently she doesn't need your help.'

'She does—she's known among her peers but not by the public.'

Leo had to curb the urge to retort that maybe they weren't missing much.

Clearly Angelica was intent on pushing the boundaries again. It wasn't even the fact that she'd cause such a stir that bothered him—after all, as he'd realised earlier, it did have its merits, her scene-stealing stunts diverting attention away from how he'd come to let everything implode so spectacularly—no, it was far more personal and prosaic. How the hell was he supposed to keep his hands off her when she was all but naked?

Angelica wondered if she'd pushed Leo too far. He had always been on the conservative side of behaviour and how he appeared in public. The opposite to Aldo. And so had she. But she had to admit that pushing her own boundaries in this situation was more thrilling than she had expected.

That's because Leo's eyes are on you. She scowled

inwardly. She knew that it wasn't for the thrill of shocking the public. It was this thrill, the way he was looking at her, as if he were about to blow a gasket.

'I can assure you that, while daring, this dress is entirely acceptable.'

Leo sounded grim. 'At least you know better than to say respectable.'

Angelica's cheeks got warm. 'Yes, well, Idrina is known for pushing the boundaries.'

Leo waved a hand in her direction. 'Pushing the boundaries, is that the name for it, then?'

Angelica rolled her eyes. 'You sound like an outdated outraged father.'

Leo's eyes met hers in a snap movement that almost felt like the sting of a whip. 'Believe me, there's nothing *fatherlike* about how I feel right now. Except perhaps for the urge to tell you to go to your room and change into something more appropriate.'

'I'm not changing. Take me, or leave me. I'd be quite happy to stay in, order takeout and watch the latest series on cable TV.'

Angelica held her breath. The tension in the air was like a live crackling force. Leo's jaw was gritted so hard, she could see a muscle bulging and had an urge to go over and put her hand on him, smoothing away the tension. That she had put there.

'Fine. Let's go, we're already late, which will ensure your entrance will be as headline-grabbing as possible.'

Angelica barely had time to grab her bag and register that he wasn't caving as he took her arm and led her out of the apartment, into the elevator and down to the lobby area, and out, to the waiting car.

She hardly noticed the chill in the air because the chill emanating from Leo on the other side of the car was more frigid. As they made their way through traffic uptown she felt him glancing at her periodically. She was very aware of her bare legs and the material barely covering the strategic middle of her body from mid-thigh, which had become upper-thigh sitting down, up to where the dress sat over her breasts.

In spite of its skimpyness, Angelica felt relatively secure. What Leo couldn't obviously see was the flesh-coloured lace that held everything in place.

'What'll be next? Just a thong?'

Angelica turned to look at Leo. His face was all harsh lines and dark brows. More stubble on his jaw. She pointed out, 'You're obviously not overly concerned with your appearance.'

He frowned. 'What's that supposed to mean?'

Before she realised what she was doing, Angelica reached out and touched a finger to his jaw, tracing the short spiky hair along his jaw-line. Too late, as her blood surged at that touch, she tried to pull her hand back but it was caught in his.

And somehow she seemed to have gravitated closer. So close that their thighs were almost touching. The air between them now felt hot and volatile. Angelica couldn't take her eyes off Leo's mouth.

His gaze was locked on her mouth too, and then it dipped down to her chest and back up again. She could see those golden depths in his eyes now. Fires burning. She wanted him to kiss her, to root her in some kind of reality even if it was an inferno. Everything had been upside down for so long...

She didn't even notice the car coming to a halt. And neither did Leo. The driver cleared his throat in the front and Leo tensed. He dropped her hand so fast it fell uselessly into her lap. She realised she was leaning towards him, her body betraying her spectacularly.

She pulled back too but Leo was already out of the car and coming around to let her out. Door opening, reaching for her hand. She'd prefer not to touch him again but it was impossible to get out of the vehicle gracefully so she had no option but to slide her hand into his, sparking a million nerve endings to life again.

They were walking up another set of steps now. Angelica was only vaguely aware of the location but it was a suitably formidable building and there was a steady stream of New York's glittering crowd entering the main door.

Paparazzi spotted them and went predictably wild, but Leo didn't want to stop. He tugged her with him until Angelica dug her heels in and he had to stop. He looked at her, his expression stormy, and bit out, 'While the news coverage isn't entirely unwelcome, I think I'd like to avoid hitting the front pages of every paper two days running.'

Angelica didn't have time to ask him what he meant by that. She said, 'I promised my friend I'd get the maximum coverage for her dress.'

Leo snorted. 'Your altruism is to be commended.

I'm sure it's nothing to do with the fact that getting photographed in little more than a lace napkin is the main aim here.'

Angelica pulled her hand free with a forced smile and made a motion to shoo Leo aside so she could be photographed on her own. To anyone else it would look like the kind of exchange that happened between celebrities on the red carpet all the time.

Angelica took her time, making sure they got all the angles and made sure they knew who the designer was. When she finally gave a wave and turned to walk up the steps, Leo practically had steam coming out of his ears.

Angelica slid her arm through his, even though that brought her uncomfortably close to his body. But she steeled herself against her reaction and said, 'If this is all too much for you, there's a very quick solution.'

'What's that?'

'A divorce.'

'Not before everything is back in my name.'

Angelica pounced. 'So you will divorce me, then, when I sign everything back to you?'

They were at the top of the steps now. Leo stopped and looked at her. 'Not a chance, not even if you decide to attend an event in nothing but body paint. We agreed to three months, and that's the minimum I'll accept to rehabilitate my image.'

Angelica swallowed down her frustration and smiled sweetly. 'It just so happens that I know a very talented body-paint artist who I've worked with on several campaigns. I must drop him an email.'

Leo urged them forward and into the event, where thousands of lights lit everyone and everything in a golden glow. Ominously he said, 'Do your worst, Angel, it won't change a thing.'

They were at the top of a set of grand marble steps that led down into a vast ballroom. Almost as one entity the crowd seemed to stop and turn to face them. A hush fell. Once again Angelica was pricklingly aware of herself. She would wear clothes like this for a shoot, no problem, but out in public was another matter. But she couldn't regret it now. He'd just confirmed she was doing the right thing. A couple of events drawing all the wrong sort of attention and he would be begging for a divorce once she'd signed everything back over to him.

Leo started walking down the stairs and she could feel his tension. She gritted her jaw against the urge to turn and flee and return in something more suitable. Did he really mean it when he said he'd make her wait out the three months? She had the sinking feeling that if she did appear in just body paint, he would call her bluff and parade her in front of everyone, rendering her little sartorial rebellions futile.

The hush became a chatter of voices that stopped and grew loud again as they passed through the crowd. People seemed to be crowding around them and in the middle of the room, Leo stopped. Angelica felt his hand tighten on hers, almost painfully, and looked up at his face and her belly swooped. He was pale and there was visible perspiration on his brow.

She squeezed his hand. 'Leo, what is it?'

His voice sounded thick. 'Need to move, get some space.'

Angelica spied an opening and moved forward, tugging Leo behind her until they'd got to the side of the ballroom, where the crowd dissipated and there was space. She turned to face him. 'Are you OK?' Theatrics with her outfits and everything was forgotten. She felt a real stab of concern. She'd never seen Leo like this.

She saw his throat swallow. A waiter passed nearby with a tray of glasses. She snagged one. Luckily it was water. She handed it to Leo. 'Drink this.'

He clasped the glass and she could see the knuckles of his fingers, white. The concern got more pronounced. He took a gulp of water and Angelica took the glass back.

'Leo?'

He shook his head. 'I'm sorry... I felt something like this at the last event but it wasn't as bad.'

'Felt what?'

'Claustrophobic. The crowd, around me...nowhere to go. Trapped.'

A chill went down Angelica's spine. 'You experienced this in prison, didn't you?'

The deathly pallor was finally lifting from his face. The faintest colour coming back. He nodded slowly. 'Something like that.'

Until now Angelica hadn't truly appreciated what he must have gone through in prison but this was giving her a glimpse.

Leo put an arm across his body as if to hold himself. Angelica instinctively moved closer and put a hand on his back. He looked at her and she saw a bleakness in his gaze for a moment that shocked her. But then it was gone. He seemed to straighten up. He took his arm down. 'I'm OK now.'

Angelica was sure he wasn't but she could read the determination in his demeanor. 'We don't have to stay, you know that. It's just a social event.'

He shook his head. 'No, we're staying.'

We. Angelica tried not to let that impact her, a sense that they were in this together, when it was anything but, but she couldn't shake it.

Leo took her hand and they skirted around the edges of the room, before she felt him literally steel himself and they moved back into the crowd. She looked at him as he conversed with a steady stream of people who came to talk to him and marvelled that unless she'd seen what had just happened—a near panic attack—he looked as vital and powerful as ever. As if it hadn't happened.

It humbled her a little. She'd endured a sort of torturous prison with Aldo but she'd managed to minimise their time together as much as possible, leaving her relatively free. Leo had been sequestered in an actual prison, where she shuddered now to think of what had happened to him to give him that reaction to being in a crowd.

Soon they were ushered into a large banquet room where an eye-wateringly long table was laid out with sparkling crockery and crystal glasses. Silver and gold cutlery. Angelica couldn't risk eating much with her outfit but in any case the food wasn't exactly meant to be eaten. It looked more like an art display. Luckily she was used to this and had eaten something earlier. She glanced at Leo, who showed no signs of his earlier stress and who was tucking into the food with enthusiasm, reminding her that he had a healthy appetite. Her cheeks got hot. For *everything*.

'You're not meant to really eat the food,' she said.

He wiped his mouth with a napkin and looked at her. 'It's delicious, you should try it.'

'I ate earlier at the shoot.' She waved her hand at herself. 'I can't really afford to dribble food down my front.'

That was a mistake. It gave licence to Leo to drop his gaze to her chest and the acreage of bare skin on display. He took his time moving his gaze back up and drawled, 'I don't think it would be all that bad.'

Instantly an image from their past came into her head. Leo spooning little blobs of ice cream onto her breasts. Specifically her nipples. She could still feel the delicious shock of the cold, followed by the even more delicious sensation of his hot mouth. Her cheeks flamed. She glared at him. He just smiled and when the person on the other side of him sought his attention, he turned away.

A couple of hours later, the dinner over and people mingling in the main ballroom again, Angelica was heartily sorry she'd ever thought of provoking Leo with her choice of clothes. People were tripping over themselves, tongues out, eyes glued to her breasts.

She had to keep resisting the urge to pull the dress down over her thighs, knowing there was no give in the fabric.

She'd been in the bathroom earlier and had overheard two women tittering about her, saying, 'She's obviously in her *exposure era*.'

The other woman had sighed then and replied, 'Well, if I had a body like that, I'd come naked.'

They'd left and Angelica had sat on the lid of the toilet for another ten minutes, hoist by her own petard and feeling increasingly uncomfortable. Especially when she thought of the fact that how she was dressed was contributing to the people crowding around them and freaking Leo out. She wanted him to see her as a liability. She didn't want to cause him stress.

You still care about him, whispered a voice. She told herself it was natural to still have feelings for someone, even if they'd rejected you. Even if they hated you for what they believed you had done to them.

Angelica was standing a little to the side near the entrance. A man had stopped Leo on their way out. He broke away now and came towards her, apologising. So different from Aldo, whose default had been total lack of consideration of anything but him.

A chill breeze made Angelica shiver lightly and Leo spotted it. He took off his jacket and draped it over her shoulders. His warmth seeped into her skin and bones, along with his scent, and Angelica had to fight not to close her eyes.

'Thank you.'

'You couldn't even bring a coat. You had to go for maximum effect.' He sounded so disapproving. And yet once again he was proving that he couldn't not be considerate.

'I forgot to think about a coat and it's been unseasonably mild,' Angelica said defensively. Until today. There was definitely a bite of winter in the air.

Leo's car pulled up and he leant forward to open the back door. Angelica got in, instinctively burrowing deeper into Leo's jacket, pulling it around her.

The journey back to the apartment was quick and uneventful. But Angelica couldn't relax. Seeing Leo so affected by being in the crowd had melted something inside her. A wall of defence. Dangerous.

Back at the apartment, Leo was still a little shaken by how quickly the sense of claustrophobia had come over him earlier and not even Angelica in her red lace excuse for a dress could have distracted him out of it. For someone who had seen some of the worst things and then experienced the foster system, Leo had always considered himself robust, but he had to admit that prison had got to him on levels he hadn't really fully acknowledged.

The lack of privacy and space. The constant danger. The sheer…hopelessness of it all. The anger and frustration. The impotency. It was all churning inside him as he opened the apartment door and let Angelica walk through.

Her scent tantalised him. She'd tantalised him all evening, once he'd got over his momentary lapse.

He'd found that having her near had definitely calmed something inside him, even if her choice of outfit had ensured that they'd been the center of attention all evening.

He was certainly back on the map. That was for sure. He watched her now as she gracefully lifted one foot behind her to slip off a shoe and then the other, lowering her height by several inches. His jacket was far too big on her. It made her look somewhat younger and fragile. It came down lower on her thighs than the dress did. He should have made her wear it all evening.

The glimpses of her curves underneath sent Leo's blood roaring through his veins.

She looked at him and her eyes had never looked so green. Bright and vibrant. But in spite of that he noticed the slight shadows underneath. Hinting that perhaps this provocative game of hers was not as straightforward as she made it seem.

She slipped the jacket off and held it out to him. 'Thanks.'

Leo stepped forward and put a hand on it, inadvertently trapping her hand. Electricity sparked between them. Neither moved to take their hands away. The moment became charged.

The control he'd had to wield all evening—to not let the crowd overwhelm him and to not let his wife send him hurtling into a volcano of need—was fraying badly.

Right now, all he could see was her and that body that had haunted his dreams and nightmares for years, covered in not much at all. In fact, she'd be less dangerous if she were naked. The fact that the red lace drew the eye to dips and hollows and plump flesh was far more provocative. The lace was strategically placed on her breasts to draw the eye—he could see the press of her nipples against the thin fabric and that made his mind blank with the need to cup that flesh and explore her with his tongue, feel the sharp tip hardening against his tongue as he drove her wild—

'Leo.'

Leo looked at her, disorientated.

'Stop looking at me like that.' Her eyes were bright. Two spots of colour in her cheeks. Mouth very red. He knew it was lipstick and he wanted to kiss it off her. Reveal their natural pink colour.

It was hard to form a coherent thought but he tried. 'Looking at you like what?'

CHAPTER FIVE

LIKE THE WAY the Big Bad Wolf would look at Little Red Riding Hood, thought Angelica. Her heart was beating so fast she could barely breathe. They were caught in a strange tableau, both still holding the jacket between them, Leo's hand on hers. Something shifted.

A longing, a yearning, rose from deep inside her. Unstoppable. It went deeper than desire, although that was there too, sharp and insistent.

She tried to pull her hand away but he tightened his hold. His gaze was on her mouth. Hungry.

'Leo…' Her voice came out low and husky, not how she'd intended at all.

'*Dio*, Angel, how you haunted me.'

'I did?'

He nodded and moved closer, tugging her to him. She went. 'How?'

'Dreams…nightmares.' His mouth tightened. 'Mainly nightmares.'

'I'm sorry,' she said helplessly. She'd had dreams and nightmares too.

'The past is gone. We're here now.'

Angelica swallowed. 'What does that mean?'

'That the present is all that matters. Moving on. And for that to happen... I can see only one way forward.'

Angelica could feel his intention as he moved closer because it echoed within her. A beating drum of desire, flames licking up and out to every extremity, making her tremble. She knew that this was a really, really bad idea but she couldn't seem to stop herself even when she knew the jacket had fallen to the floor and Leo was wrapping his hands around her waist, pulling her even closer.

'Did you really think I could see you dressed like that and maintain some kind of illusion that I was in control?'

'I didn't dress like this for that...'

His mouth twisted a little, 'No, you did it to irritate the hell out of me and make me look like a fool.'

Angelica thought of his pale face and the fear in his eyes earlier. It had thrown her, made her heart squeeze with concern, but she couldn't deny that irritating him *had* been her intention. But now her reasoning for it all felt a bit hazy. 'Yes,' she agreed simply. And then, before he could say anything else, she said, 'But I'm sorry that it brought more attention... I didn't know that you...' She trailed off.

'Neither did I,' he said. 'But I don't want to talk about that now. I don't want to talk at all.'

Neither did she. When Leo lowered his head to hers, she tipped her face up, telling him that she wanted him. His mouth hovered over hers for a long moment and Angelica's hands went to his shirt, fingers clutching at the material. She was about to pull him closer in a bid to close the gap when those firm contours that she remembered so well settled over hers.

Her legs instantly felt weak and she had to lock her knees to stay standing. Apart from the shock of being kissed by Leo again, the yearning emotion caught at her gut. It felt as if she was coming home. And that was so disturbing and disconcerting that she opened her mouth to him, so the kiss could deepen and become much more explicit. Leo wasted no time in matching her, showing her so effortlessly who was the master here.

She was drowning in sensations and needs and when Leo pulled back after long drugging minutes, it was hard for Angelica to open her eyes and when she did he was out of focus.

He was looking at her, her face caught in his hands. He wiped his thumbs across her tender mouth and said, 'That's better.'

She wasn't even sure what he was referring to, only that she wanted his hands on her bare flesh. She'd felt cold for so long and, finally, heat was reaching all the way into the deepest part of her and spreading out.

'Leo, please…'

'Do you want me?'

She nodded. 'Yes.' There was no hesitation. She'd never thought she'd be here again with him, like this. With him looking at her like this. The last time she'd seen him…there had been such coldness in his eyes. Voice. In a bid to banish the memories,

Angelica reached up and pressed her mouth to his, showing him.

It was like setting a match to dry kindling that was already burning. His arms and hands were wrapped so tight around her, he was lifting her off the floor and Angelica was not a small woman.

Her breasts were crushed to his chest, thighs pressing together. She felt his erection against the juncture of her legs and she moved against him as a sense of desperation mounted.

He dragged his mouth away and she heard him curse. She let out a small laugh. For the first time in three years, something light and effervescent bubbled up inside her.

Leo dipped slightly and caught her under her legs and carried her through the apartment to his bedroom. She hadn't been in here. It was vast with windows taking in the night view—Manhattan lit up like a bauble under a clear night sky. They were floating above it all as if in some kind of cocoon. He put her down by the bed and looked at her. Impatient, she reached for his bow tie and undid it, pulling it off, fingers finding and undoing his buttons.

He stood there and let her open his shirt, push it back and let it slide off his body. She looked at his chest, eyes greedy to see him again. The perfect musculature, the golden skin. She reached out a hand but just as she did something caught her eye and she stopped breathing.

A nasty scar, just under his ribs. Jagged. It hadn't been there before. Instinctively, she moved her hand down and touched it lightly with her fingers. She heard Leo's indrawn breath and looked up. 'What happened?'

He put his hand over hers and lifted it away gently. 'Let's just say it was an early lesson in where I came in the pecking order in prison. They don't think much of white collar crime.'

Angelica felt her eyes prickle at the thought of such violence being meted out to this man, who hadn't deserved it for a second. All while Aldo had been creating havoc. She couldn't look at him, for fear he'd see the emotion in her eyes. 'I'm sorry.'

'You didn't stab me.'

Maybe not, but he still thought she was complicit with Aldo and therefore responsible on some level. The urge to make him understand how sorry she was and that she'd had nothing to do with it all made her open her mouth but Leo put a finger to her lips, stopping her words before they'd even formulated.

'No more talking, it's not important now.'

Angelica swallowed her words. Leo put his hands to his trousers and undid the belt and top button.

'Let me,' she said, replacing his hands with hers and pulling the zip down over the hard bulge. Her blood was boiling in her veins. His trousers fell to the ground. He stepped out of them. Angelica hooked her fingers into the sides of his underwear and pulled it down. His erection sprang free and her legs almost buckled again. He was as magnificent as she remembered. A potent, virile male in his prime.

She only noticed her hand was shaking when she

reached out to touch him, fingers tracing the veins that ran along the shaft. She heard another indrawn breath, more like a hiss. He caught her hand again and said thickly, 'I won't last if you keep touching me like that.'

Angelica let her hand drop and looked up at him, then she turned around. 'There's a zip in the material at the back.' In the flesh-coloured fine mesh that held the dress in place.

But Leo didn't put his fingers on the zip, she felt him undoing her hair, pulling out the tie and then letting it fall before furrowing his fingers into her hair and onto her scalp, massaging it. She groaned softly. It was bliss.

He said from behind her, 'I never forgot how your hair feels like silk.' Then, he swept it over one shoulder and found the cleverly hidden zip, although at this point Angelica wouldn't have objected if he'd ripped the fabric asunder. But he took his time, pulling the zip down to just above her buttocks. She pulled free of the arms of the dress—designed to make it look as if it were sleeveless—and pulled down the body, over her hips and down all the way. She wore no bra, only a thong. The dress had precluded wearing anything underneath.

She hadn't been naked in front of anyone since Leo. Not even Aldo had managed to get that far. Thank God. Angelica shuddered a little just at the thought.

'You're cold.'

She turned around and shook her head. 'No.' But what she was, was nervous. It made her bring her arms up to cover her breasts. Leo had said she'd lost weight, maybe he wouldn't find her attractive any more.

But he caught her arms and pulled them apart gently. She could feel his eyes on her and her heart stuttered.

He said reverently, 'I thought… I'd dreamt you up. That maybe you'd never really existed…that such beauty couldn't be possible.'

Angelica looked up. 'I'm just flesh and blood… there's a million women out there who are infinitely more alluring than I am.'

Leo shook his head. 'I don't think so. Come here.'

He pulled her towards him until their bodies were touching. Every part of Angelica's skin prickled with anticipation. Need.

He kissed her again and she fell into it, twining her arms around his neck and bringing their bodies even closer. His hands were smoothing up and down her back, her waist, hips, fingers tugging her underwear down and off.

Now, cupping one breast and squeezing the firm flesh. Angelica pulled back, breathing heavily. 'I need you, Leo…now.'

She could only read the stark need she felt mirrored on his face and it buoyed something inside her. In this…they were equal. No messy past, no tense present, no uncertain future. Just *now*.

Somehow, he manoeuvred them to the bed and Angelica tumbled back, looking up at Leo. He was so tall and proud and powerful, and yet she could imagine that even he hadn't been a match for a gang in the prison, intent on showing him who was master of that domain. Certainly not him.

The lurid scar hovered on the edge of her vision and made her feel emotional again. She reached out her arms. 'Leo...'

He made a move towards her and then stopped, cursing softly. 'I need to get protection...'

He'd turned and was walking towards the en suite before Angelica could get a word out to tell him she was protected. Still protected. She'd gone on the pill during their brief affair and she'd stayed on it through the marriage to Aldo, terrified that if things changed and he hadn't been inhibited sexually by her, that he might force her into his bed...and the thought of that, and possibly a baby... Angelica couldn't countenance such a thing, so she'd made sure she was protected.

Leo was still in the bathroom. Angelica felt a slight draught from somewhere skate over her skin. She came up on one elbow. 'Leo?'

'Leo?'

He heard her asking for him and every single cell in his body was straining to return, wanting to obey the drumbeat of need in his blood. But Leo had just caught sight of his reflection in the mirror and couldn't move.

His expression was stark. He looked almost fevered. Eyes glittering with hunger. Jaw tight with need. Muscles bunching, taut. His head was filled with the image of *her*, as she'd lain on the bed just now. Long limbs, soft curves. Dark hair spread out on white sheets. Dark, sharp nipples, asking for his tongue to surround them and make them even sharper.

Curls at the juncture of her legs where he could remember how she'd felt when he'd entered her, how she'd moulded around him so tightly, sending his mind into orbit.

It struck him like a slap across the face. He was about to dive back into the fire that had almost consumed him three years ago, leading him down a path where he'd almost forgotten who he was and where he'd come from. What he'd witnessed, the senseless brutal murder of his entire family at the hands of a rogue Mafia goon, high on drugs and calling in a debt. Trying to impress his peers. That's when Leo had vowed to himself—to never be in a position where he had to watch everyone he loved be destroyed again.

Angelica had told him she loved him. But it had been a lie. When he'd rejected her, she'd gone from him straight into his best friend's bed. Together they'd betrayed him. And yet here he was about to forget the three years of purgatory they—she—had inflicted on him? The knife scar itched, as if her touch had brought those awful moments back to life, when he'd been surrounded, unable to move and then he'd felt a sharp, inexplicable pain, followed by intense heat and shock. Blood everywhere. Men backing away laughing. 'Now you have real blood on your hands.'

But their faces morphed into hers. She must be laughing at him, at how easily he was forgetting his outrage. How quickly he was opening his arms to her again. How weak he was. He went cold inside, the flames of desire doused by a reality check.

Leo stood up straight and grabbed a towel, lashing it around his waist and tying it. He went to the door and opened it. Angelica was on the other side, wearing his shirt, holding it together with one hand. She looked concerned. 'Are you OK?'

Leo forced down the heat he could already feel pooling deep down, just at the sight of her in his shirt, knowing she had nothing underneath, hair tumbled around her shoulders. That beautiful sexy mouth plump from his kisses.

Dio. Before he could change his mind, he said, 'I think you should go back to your room. This was a mistake.'

It took a second for Leo's words to register but when they did, Angelica felt them in her gut, like a physical blow. She was winded. Almost felt like doubling over. *Of course*, rang in her head. Of course he had planned this. How to humiliate her with maximum effect. Get her on her back, naked, begging him...and then...slap her aside.

She took a step back, clutching the shirt to her chest, glad she'd put it on at the last minute. She'd been concerned. Leo had been in the bathroom for long minutes. Her concern mocked her now. Had she learnt nothing?

She heard herself say, 'Why?' Even though she knew the answer.

Leo's face was tight. Eyes dark. 'It's just... I wasn't thinking. This isn't a good idea.'

A little harsh laugh came out of Angelica's mouth before she could stop it. 'Oh, you were thinking all right. You knew exactly what you were doing, but you've done us both a favour. You're right, this isn't a good idea.'

She turned before he could see the emotion rising to choke her and went to the door of the bedroom, pulling it open. From behind her he said, 'Angel, wait... I didn't intend to do this...like this.'

Angelica didn't turn around. She said, 'You didn't used to be a bastard, Leo, but maybe you've changed, like I have.'

She walked out.

Leo had slept badly. Angel's words reverberated in his head all night. *You didn't used to be a bastard.* His conscience pricked. He could see how it might look to her, but he hadn't set out to seduce her and then reject her.

But he couldn't have trusted that she was sleeping with him with no agenda. Especially after what had happened.

Except she hadn't looked as if she had an agenda. She'd looked as if he'd punched her. The colour leaching from her face. Eyes wide. *Hurt.* They'd reminded him of her expression that morning in Venice, when he'd told her to leave. After she'd declared she loved him.

But that had been an act, in league with Aldo, he

asserted, even though it suddenly felt a lot less easy to believe.

Maybe subconsciously he had wanted to expose her, humiliate her, but he knew the bigger motivation had been the speed at which he'd forgotten everything and just wanted her. Needed her.

Dio. Where was she? They had to leave for Rome shortly. If she didn't appear in the dining room in the next five— There was a noise at the door and Leo looked up from his paper that he hadn't been reading.

She stood in the doorway, dressed in dark trousers and a dark long-sleeved top. Flat shoes. Hair pulled back into a knot. A million miles from the sorceress in the barely there red lace dress that had almost tempted him over the edge. A voice mocked him now. *Would it have been so bad? Even if she had laughed at you?*

He stood up. 'There's a few minutes for breakfast. Do you want something hot?'

She didn't meet his eye as she came in and took a seat at the other end of the table. Michael appeared with a coffee pot and cup and put them down. She looked at him and smiled. 'Thank you, Michael.'

'No problem.'

When Michael had left Leo watched her pour herself some coffee. His insides were tight. She looked pale, a little drawn.

'Angel, I—'

She looked at him and her face was a smooth expressionless mask. 'Please, don't call me that. And if you're going to say anything in reference to what happened last night, please don't, there's nothing to discuss.'

The tension throbbing between them begged otherwise but Leo took her cue. For now. 'Fine, we leave in five minutes, OK?'

She just nodded and took another sip of coffee.

Angelica was aware of Leo across the aisle of the plane but she was doing her damndest not to be. To her mortification last night, she'd gone straight into her shower, turned it on to hot and had cried like a baby.

It hadn't just been the humiliation of Leo's rejection, it had been three years of pent-up stress and emotion. The grief she'd never really expressed for the end of their relationship.

She'd meant what she'd said. The Leo she'd known would never have done something so cruel. But then, when she'd known him he'd been an idealistic young man, revelling in his success without being arrogant or complacent, eager to make a good mark on the world. Half of his ambitions had had to do with philanthropy as much as achieving personal success.

No wonder she'd fallen so hard for him.

Now, he *was* different, and that scar marking where he'd been stabbed was just the tip of the iceberg. Maybe prison had also taught him to be cruel. Vindictive. Vengeful.

And yet, he hadn't looked triumphant last night, as if he'd got her where he wanted her, rejected and humiliated. He'd looked a little…shaken. As if maybe he'd looked in the mirror and seen something. Or, remembered that he hated her and shouldn't debase himself by touching her.

In any case, he'd done them a favour. He'd reminded her of what was at stake. Her family's safety. After last night, she knew she had even less reason to trust him. And to think that she'd almost wanted to blurt out a defence—to tell him that she hadn't been complicit with Aldo. By revealing everything. That made any sense of humiliation fade into insignificance.

Since she'd met Leo again—since he'd ambushed her, kidnapped her—she'd been running to catch up, get her breath. Revealing too much. Reacting. Provoking. When what she really needed to do was retreat into the space she'd inhabited when she'd been with Aldo, where nothing could touch her, or harm her. Where she was numb.

She'd done it for three years, to survive. She could do it for another few months.

The journey from the private airfield just outside Rome into the city was silent. As silent as the plane journey had been. All eight hours twenty minutes of it. Leo knew, he'd felt every minute. Admittedly, Angelica had slept for almost half of it, curled up on the seat across from him, refusing his suggestion to use the bedroom with a curt shake of her head.

Once again she hadn't met his eye. It was disconcerting because he knew she wasn't sulking. Or being petulant. It was literally as if he weren't there. Or consequential.

He'd put a cashmere throw over her as she'd slept, and had had to sit down again before his fingers had traced the smooth curve of her cheek, lashes long and dark.

You could have touched her all over last night, but you didn't. He didn't have a right to touch her. *You didn't used to be a bastard.*

Leo spoke now to break the silence as much as anything else. 'We're going straight to my legal team's offices. They're working late especially for us.'

'OK.'

The first time Leo had heard her voice since this morning. He gritted his jaw and looked out of the window. It was as if she had retreated behind some invisible wall.

When they arrived at the offices, she was out of the car by the time Leo reached her door. Sending a strong signal to keep back. He put out a hand to indicate for her to precede him into the sleek building, gritting his jaw even harder.

Maybe this froideur was all a precursor to this moment when she would reveal that she wasn't so sanguine about letting Aldo's wealth go, after all. Right now, Leo almost welcomed that scenario, as if it would salve his conscience. But somehow, he had a feeling that Angelica would confound him again, as she'd been doing from the very start.

Angelica signed the last piece of paper. There was a hush in the office. She could sense Leo behind her, eyes boring into her upper back. His surprise was palpable.

'Can I get some water, please?' she asked.

About three assistants scrambled to get her water. She almost smiled when she heard a soft curse behind her and then a familiar scent washed over her and a strong masculine hand was putting down a glass of water on the table by her elbow.

'I'm sorry, you shouldn't have had to ask.'

Angelica took a sip and saw one assistant's face go pale, clearly under Leo's fierce look of censure.

She figured he might not be so accommodating if she'd kicked up a fuss over signing away any last links to Aldo's money. But of course she hadn't. Now she really was free of his toxic tentacles.

She stood up and the solicitors, lawyers and assistants melted away. She turned around to face Leo, who was looking at her a little warily. She'd been avoiding looking at him for most of the day and now he filled her vision.

Tall and broad, light blue shirt, dark trousers. Top button open. Sleeves rolled up. Hair messy. Jaw stubbled.

She wished she hadn't looked at him because now she couldn't look away and the humiliation of the previous night came flooding back. She clung onto her impassive shell, loath to let Leo see how he affected her.

Eventually he said almost accusingly, 'I don't get it. Why did you marry him if it wasn't for his money or power?'

Angelica went over to one of the windows. Night had fallen outside. The city was lit up. She could see the outline of the Colosseum in the distance. She could also see Leo reflected in the window behind her. She felt brittle and exposed. 'You're so cynical. Maybe we were in love.' She nearly choked on the words.

He made a snorting sound. 'Yes, your grief is admirable.'

Angelica turned around, arms folded across her chest. 'It's none of your business. You dumped me, remember? You don't get to know about my life after that.'

Leo frowned. 'Did you go with him to get back at me?'

Angelica almost laughed at the quaint notion. But then she just felt incredibly weary. 'No, I did not marry that man to punish you for rejecting me.'

Leo opened his mouth again but Angelica put up a hand, 'I'm quite tired now. It's been a long day. Where are we staying?'

'I'm renting an apartment in a hotel not far from here. Aldo sold the apartment I had here under the company name. I'm looking at properties to buy.'

Angelica's insides twisted. She'd loved Leo's Rome apartment, high in one of the oldest buildings with an outdoor terrace that gave 360-degree views of the ancient city. She'd known that Aldo had sold it and when he'd crowed about it she'd just looked right through him and pretended she couldn't care less.

Leo said, 'I'm going to stay here and do a little bit of work. We have a charity function to attend tomorrow evening at the art museum. This is our first appearance in Rome. I'm sure you'll make it as memorable as our appearances in New York.'

That weariness washed over Angelica again. The thought of seeking out the most outrageous outfit to wear was no longer remotely appealing. She was eternally grateful when Leo said, 'The driver is downstairs. He'll take you to the hotel. I'll see you in the morning.'

She didn't respond, she just walked out, feeling both lighter for having signed away any right to Aldo's tainted legacy and heavy, to be back here in Rome with the man who had made her both happier than she'd ever thought she could be, and more devastated.

When she got to the sumptuous apartment at the top of one of Rome's most exclusive hotels, she blindly went into the first empty bedroom she found, pulled off her clothes and tried not to think of Leo undoing her zip on that dress last night. She took a shower and crawled into the bed with the robe still on and fell into a deep sleep.

Even though he'd told Angelica that he wanted to work, Leo couldn't settle after she'd left. Things just weren't adding up. *Why* hadn't she demanded some of Aldo's fortune? Which, admittedly, was all Leo's. She could have named her price and Leo would have given it to her in order to own his own business outright again. But she'd just signed every piece of paper handed to her. Much as she had in New York.

Of course it had occurred to him over the years that, in a fit of pique at his rejection, she'd flitted into the arms of his best friend, but not really until now, until it had become clear she had no designs on taking anything for herself. Which she was entitled to.

She'd even point-blank refused a percentage of what she had inherited on Aldo's death. She'd almost looked ill at the suggestion.

Leo stood at the window in the same spot where she'd stood. No, things were not clear at all, and now that she had effectively signed everything back over to him...could he really insist that they remain married?

He thought of the press coverage, especially after *that* dress last night. The dress that had pushed him over the edge of his reason. The dress that had appeared splashed over every tabloid from New York to London.

No, he still needed her. If she wasn't providing such a distraction, the press would be all over his current situation and asking questions and speculating as to how he could have possibly been weak enough as to almost lose everything. And, could it happen again? He knew not, but he needed to be in a strong position of power when eyes turned to him again. He didn't want there to be any doubt that he would ever risk his company again.

As of this evening, it was returned to his name and with a new title: Falzone Global Management. He was back on track, a bit bruised and scarred but otherwise intact.

He should just accept the fact that she had chosen not to contest her inheritance and move on. Maybe she was that proud and independent. Far more than he'd even given her credit for. She still owed him for her betrayal and, as she'd pointed out, maybe it was none of his business what her motives were. She'd given him what he wanted and he would make use of her until he was ready to let her go.

Last night he'd almost forgotten everything. He wouldn't make that mistake again. Even if Angelica turned up naked to the next event.

CHAPTER SIX

ANGELICA WOKE THE next morning to a low buzzing sound. She kept her eyes closed, relishing the soft cocoon of the bed. She felt disorientated and images came back—signing legal papers, *Leo*, maintaining a cool and icy distance that had taken more out of her than she had admitted to herself.

Somehow it was much harder to do around Leo than it had been with Aldo. *Because you never wanted Aldo.* She eventually opened her eyes with a scowl on her face and blinked, looking around.

Sounds from the street far below trickled up through an open window. Curtains fluttering gently in the breeze. *Rome.* Then that humming noise again coming from a doorway on the other side of the room.

Angelica pushed back the covers and got out of the bed, pulling the robe around her tightly. She approached the door and opened it and her eyes widened on the sight of Leo—bare-chested, with nothing but a small towel slung around his waist.

He was shaving and he stopped and looked at her. She asked, 'What are you doing here?'

'You slept in my bed last night. All my things are in this bathroom. It was just easier to come here.'

Angelica looked behind her into the room and saw things she hadn't noticed last night. A man's watch on the nightstand. Books. A clock. A suit-bag hanging from a wardrobe door. This robe that she was wearing, which was too big.

Her face got hot. 'I'm sorry, I just came in and had a shower and went straight to bed. I didn't think…'

'It's fine, I took the guest room.'

'I'll move there this morning.'

'You can stay if you like, I don't mind.'

That just brought up images of her and Leo in the same bed, waking up…as they'd used to, entwined.

'I'll go and get some coffee.' She needed to wake up.

'Breakfast should have been delivered by now.'

Angelica fled, without looking at Leo again. When she emerged into the dining area there were some hotel staff who greeted her deferentially and then left.

They'd left a breakfast spread of hot food, and pastries. Fruit and granola. And coffee. Angelica poured a cup and took a sip, hoping that would restore some sense of equilibrium.

For a moment there, finding Leo in the bathroom had felt far too much like déjà vu.

'Have you any plans for the day?'

Angelica jolted slightly. She must have been lost in a daydream for long minutes. Leo was there, clean-shaven, wearing a three-piece suit. Every inch the successful financier. His business restored. She couldn't deny that he deserved that.

But she strove to maintain that cool front. 'I have some personal admin to do.'

Leo sat down and helped himself to coffee and a big portion of hot food. That reminder of his healthy appetite. Not welcome. She wondered if he'd been with anyone since being released from prison. She hadn't been with anyone since him. And now she was glad he'd come to his senses last night because the thought of him realising that he was still her one and only lover...made her squirm with a sense of exposure.

'I also have to go to my agent's office. They have some upcoming jobs they want to discuss.'

Leo said, 'I can drop you on my way to my office if you like.'

Angelica shook her head. 'No, it's fine, I'd like the walk.'

'Did Aldo like your independence?'

It took a second for Angelica to register Leo's question. She looked at him and said coolly, 'He had no choice.'

'I'm glad he didn't diminish that.'

Angelica felt a surge of emotion to hear Leo say that. To acknowledge that he remembered how important her independence was to her. Ever since she'd left Sicily she'd been conscious of providing for her mother and brother, and then, taking on the bigger responsibility of getting them out of harm's way. She was proud of how she'd been able to do all of that off the back of her earnings. A mere trifle compared to

Leo's fortune, but no less significant for that. After losing her father, and with her leaving Sicily, she'd always felt as if she'd abandoned them so to be able to do something for them had been amazing. And that had been her whole focus, until Leo had come along and sent her world into a spin. And now he was sending it into a spin all over again.

Terrified he'd notice the chink in her armour, Angelica stood up and grabbed a pastry, along with her coffee. 'I have to get ready, I'll see you later.'

Just before she got to the door, Leo said from behind her, 'I'll arrange for a team to be here to help you get ready for the event.'

'OK, fine.' And she slipped out of the room and made sure she used the guest suite this time. Although, it didn't help that she noticed the crumpled bed sheets and felt an almost overwhelming urge to press her face into the pillow to smell his scent.

That evening Leo waited in the living area. He was dressed in his tuxedo. The glam team had left shortly before. He hated to admit it but he felt an illicit frisson at the thought of what Angelica might wear for this evening.

When she did appear, he almost felt a spurt of disappointment. She was covered from neck to toe. A black dress, very elegant and classic. Her hair was slicked back and left loose down her back. Discreet diamond jewellery. Positively demure.

'I'm ready.'

Leo looked at her face. That cool impenetrable

mask she'd been wearing since the previous night was still in place. It made him want to go over and take her face in his hands and kiss her, or do something to bring back the spark. *No.*

'OK, let's go.'

It was only when they were walking through the lobby to his car outside and Leo noticed heads swivelling in their direction that he looked down and noticed that Angelica's dress had a slit on one side, giving an eyeful of one long, sleek, toned leg as she walked. Almost all the way up to her underwear. And that the dress was made of some kind of semi-sheer clinging material.

Not so demure after all. The ever-kindling spark inside him burst into flame. It was going to be a long evening.

Angelica's face was sore from fake smiling as people came up to greet her and Leo. She'd been aware of his tension in the crowd and hated that she was. Hated that she cared. But he didn't seem to be exhibiting the same signs of stress as before.

No one mentioned Aldo. It was as if he'd never existed. He hadn't ever really been welcome among Rome's high society in any case. He'd used Angelica in a bid to make himself seem less…connected to a dubious past. Something Leo had never had to worry about. He'd never hid where he came from but he'd also taken great pains to distance himself from any association with Sicily's darker side.

Aldo hadn't. Maybe if Leo had taken more notice

of that he might not have trusted Aldo so much. Angelica had never much taken to him, while she'd been with Leo. She'd never liked the way his eyes moved over her, as if she were a piece of meat. And he would invade her space, as if to provoke a reaction. But she'd always stood her ground with him, staring him down until he was the one to break.

And when they'd married, she'd discovered that that had all been bluster. When it came to it, the man had been a coward.

But, she didn't want to think about him now because she had something potentially very exciting happening, which could lead to her arranging a secret meeting with her family. A job in Madrid, where they lived, on the outskirts of the city. Surely she could arrange a trip on her own without causing Leo to suspect anything?

When the next person came up to talk to Leo, Angelica smiled for real this time, at the thought that within the next twenty-four hours she might see and hug her mother and brother. Even if it was just a short meeting, it would sustain her, because clearly, even though she'd proven that she wanted nothing of Leo's business or fortune, he was determined to have his pound of flesh. His three months of revenge.

'That's better.'

Angelica looked up as Leo's arm snaked around her waist, pulling her into him and emptying her mind of anything rational. Damn him. Her smile faded.

'No, don't go back into robot mode. You were looking human again for a second.'

'I don't know what you're talking about.'

Leo sighed audibly and took her hand, expertly moving them to the side of the vast ballroom. He stopped and stood in front of her. She couldn't help but notice that he made sure he was still facing the crowd, that no one was at his back. Angelica pulled her hand away. It felt too nice. Too disturbing. This man had humiliated her in the worst way and she'd never forgive him for that.

'Angel…'

She looked up at him, 'Don't call me that.'

He scowled, but then said, 'Angelica. I want to say something about last night—'

She went to turn to walk back into the crowd. 'Well, I don't.'

He caught her arm, stopping her. 'Please.'

She eventually turned back to face him, focusing on his bow tie.

'Look, last night… I didn't intend to do that, to stop. I wanted you, I *want* you. We both know it'd be a lie to deny that.'

Angelica swallowed and did her best to ignore the ominous prickling at the back of her eyes. 'You don't have to say anything.'

'I do. You know I'm not like that. I wouldn't lead someone on only to reject them, out of some sense of spite or cruelty.'

She lifted her eyes to his, feeling very vulnerable. 'So, why?'

He sighed again. 'Because I felt exposed.'

'I was exposed too.'

He nodded. 'I know. I'm sorry. You didn't deserve that.'

Angelica hadn't expected that. It broke something apart inside her. Another piece of the wall she'd built to survive.

He said now, 'I don't trust you...not after everything that happened. But I still want you.'

'I don't trust you either.' Except, Angelica had to admit that her lack of trust was probably a lot shakier than his. He had more reason not to trust her.

'We don't need to trust each other to want each other.'

The thought of putting herself out there again, after last night, made her go cold. 'We might want each other, Leo, but you were right, last night was a mistake.'

'I think it was a mistake...to stop.'

Angelica's heart beat faster. The noise of the crowd around them faded. All she could see were his eyes and the golden flames in the dark depths.

Then he said, 'I haven't been with anyone, since you.'

Another piece of the wall crumbled. Angelica shook her head, even as she could feel her body subtly moving closer to Leo. 'I won't let you humiliate me again.' That was twice now. When he'd dumped her on that fateful day three years ago, and last night.

'I won't.'

'No, you won't, because you won't get that chance.'

'Never say never, Angel.'

'I told you not to—'

'*There* you are, Leo. We've been looking all over for you…'

The voice came from behind her. The interruption stalled Angelica's words in her throat. Leo looked at her and all but smirked. He took her hand and slid his fingers through hers. It felt shockingly intimate. He wouldn't let her pull away but the worst of it was that she didn't want to.

She hadn't seen this side of him since they'd met again and it was seductive. And she knew that if he really turned on the charm, he'd be nigh on impossible to resist.

It was how he'd persuaded her to go out with him the first time. She'd been focused solely on her career, no interest in a romantic relationship, too invested in making enough money to support herself and her mother and brother—plus, she'd never met anyone who'd remotely interested her—and then Leonardo Falzone had appeared at her agent's office asking them to send her a message on his behalf.

She'd been there for a meeting and had recognised him as soon as she'd seen him across the room. The man she'd bumped into a few evenings before at the function, when her drink had spilled all over her dress. She hadn't been able to get his beautiful face out of her head. Or, the way something about him had piqued her interest.

She'd told her agent to go ahead and give him her number. He'd called almost straight away…

'Let's dance.'

Angelica blinked and looked up, past and present

merging for a second, making her feel a little dizzy. The person talking to Leo had left and now he was tugging her around the edge of the room to the dance floor.

She asked, 'How are you...in the crowd?'

He seemed OK but she did notice little lines of tension around his mouth. He nodded. 'Much better.' He looked down at her as he swung her into his arms, and her body collided gently with his, all of her softness pressing against his much harder form. He said again with emphasis, '*Much* better.'

Angelica wanted to groan softly but she held it back and tried to remain rigid in Leo's arms but it was next to impossible. She'd been holding herself rigid for so long that her body longed to just...flow and relax. And as if he could sense that, Leo seemed hell-bent on accommodating her body's wishes.

Feeling angry now that Leo seemed intent on dismantling all of her defences, Angelica looked up at him, gaze skipping off the danger of his mouth and up to his eyes. 'How can you want me when you hate me?'

He stopped dancing for a moment and looked down at her. A fleeting expression crossed his face, unguarded, but too fast for her to decipher it.

'I don't...hate you.'

And, Angelica realised, she didn't hate Leo. Not even after he couldn't love her, because he'd never promised that. Not even after he wanted to punish her. What she did feel was tangled and complicated and too much to think about right now.

But as if a little devil had taken control, she heard herself blurting out, 'Why did you dump me?'

He tensed. She felt it. He said after a long moment, 'Because I never promised you anything more than what we had. I didn't want a long-term commitment.'

She stayed silent. As if the words were being dragged out of him, he said, 'You know my background, so similar to yours. I never wanted a relationship, family. When you said…what you said, I knew things had gone too far.'

Too far. Meaning she'd lost the run of herself and had been building happy-ever-after castles in the air. It was small comfort that she knew Leo didn't believe she'd meant it when she'd told him she loved him, and the last thing she needed now was him reflecting on that. But before she could say anything to deflect him, he was saying, 'No, I don't hate you, Angelica, but I do want you.'

They'd started dancing again, which was causing a far too distracting friction between their bodies. Especially considering that Angelica's dress was gossamer thin. She could hardly deny she wanted him—it was out in the open now, like an electric current that couldn't be switched off. Any attempt to maintain a cool facade was fast melting like snow on a hot stone.

Almost as if musing aloud, Leo looked down at her and said, 'You say it's not my business but I think it is.'

Angelica was having trouble thinking straight. 'Your business about what?'

'Why you went to Aldo if it wasn't to get back at me or get your hands on his, that is, *my*, money.'

Angelica's brain was suddenly crystal clear again. She could feel herself tensing. She really didn't want Leo going down this route of looking at her motives because she had no defence except the truth about her family and now that she was so close to seeing them she really didn't want to jeopardise anything.

Instead of an answer she couldn't give, she said, 'Now that you have everything back in your name, are you sure you don't want to divorce and be rid of me?'

Leo pulled her closer as a couple nearly collided with them, and when they'd passed by he didn't loosen his hold. Angelica was sure she could feel every ridge of every muscle, and one in particular, hardening against her. She flushed.

Leo seemed oblivious to what was happening below their necks but she could see the heated look in his eyes. He shook his head. 'Three months minimum. You've proved to be very valuable at diverting attention away from the danger of speculation as to my ability to protect myself from future attack.'

Angelica couldn't begrudge Leo this. Even if it did mean her little plan to attract the wrong sort of attention had backfired spectacularly. And thankfully he wasn't insisting she tell him the truth of her reasons for marrying Aldo.

'I'll start dressing like a nun.'

'No doubt that'll only send them into further paroxysms of delight. There's nothing you could wear that would dim your beauty or sensuality.'

Angelica's insides flipped. This man was the one who had opened her eyes to her own sensuality. She'd never considered herself a very sexual person until she'd slept with him. He'd awoken something primal inside her and she could feel it now, clawing for release. It had been so long.

Feeling a little exposed all over again, she said, 'Careful, that almost sounds like a compliment.'

'You don't need me to tell you how beautiful you are.'

Angelica shook her head. 'I'm well aware that I'm lucky enough to photograph well and fit into the current beauty parameters but there are far more beautiful than me.' She looked to her side and said, 'See that woman there?'

Leo looked. 'The older woman, with the grey hair?'

Angelica nodded. 'She's stunning. You can tell she's had no work done. All of those beautiful lines on her face tell the story of a life lived. She looks happy.'

'Were you always such a romantic?'

Angelica's face got hot. She was losing it. Proximity to Leo was scrambling her brain cells. This time when she pulled back he let her go. 'I need the bathroom.'

She walked off the dance floor, aware of looks and whispers as she went. She felt a little unsteady, as if she were on a ship. When she got to the bathroom she sat in a stall and got her breath back.

She had been a romantic. Right up until he'd told her their relationship was over. And then Aldo and his toxic cruelty had further eroded any belief in romance. But it hadn't been fully decimated in spite of everything that had happened and now Leo was seeing right inside her to where she was still vulnerable. And that was a shock, to fully acknowledge how much she still hoped, and wanted for *more*. How she wanted to imagine a life with someone again, having a family full of love and security. Longevity. Growing old together. Not cut short by violence. A life full of meaning and satisfaction, in the small everyday things. Nothing outrageous.

Perhaps it was the prospect of finally getting to see her mother and brother, exposing her vulnerabilities. But she knew it wasn't. It was him.

Something had shifted between her and Leo. She hadn't been expecting him to apologise for last night. To admit that he'd felt exposed. She couldn't arm herself against him when he was like this.

But she had to. If she slept with him, she'd never be able to protect herself and emerge from this marriage arrangement intact.

He'd broken her heart into a million pieces once already. She wouldn't survive if he did it again.

Steeling herself to go back to Leo and try to ignore the pull between them, she wasn't expecting to see him waiting outside the bathroom. He was leaning against a wall and stood up as she approached. He said, 'I'm ready to go, do you mind?'

Angelica felt relieved. She shook her head. 'Not at all.' She didn't miss the way Leo still had that heated look in his eyes. She would ignore it. Go straight to bed when they returned. In the guest suite. Which had been cleaned by staff earlier. So she wouldn't have to worry about his scent on the sheets.

When they went outside, Leo took his jacket off and gave it to her, settling it over her shoulders. His warmth seeped under her skin. She gritted her jaw and she said *thank you*. He knew exactly what he was doing.

When they got back to the apartment in the hotel, Angelica avoided looking at Leo as she slipped off his jacket and handed it back to him, very careful in case he tried anything. But he just took it without touching her hand.

She looked at him, suddenly feeling foolish, as if perhaps she'd just imagined the crackling chemistry between them, but as soon as she took one look at his face and eyes she knew she hadn't imagined it.

He wanted her. Exactly as he'd told her.

He said, 'There's no reason why this can't be a marriage in the bedroom too. We want each other... clearly there's unfinished business.'

Angelica straightened up. 'If you don't mind, I think I'd prefer to take my chances and let unfinished business remain unfinished. There were plenty of women at that event who I'm sure would be only too happy to accommodate your...needs. After all, it never stopped Aldo.' Her husband might not have been able to perform with her—thank God—but he'd been perfectly capable with others.

And she only realised the impact and meaning of what she'd just said when Leo frowned. 'Is that what happened? He was unfaithful?' He issued a curse word.

If Leo thought she'd been unhappy in her marriage with Aldo because of infidelity then she'd have to leave it at that. She couldn't explain the truth. *You could try.* Her heart beat fast at the thought of telling him everything but then the fear returned. She couldn't yet trust that he wouldn't use her family to get back at her. And she was so close to seeing them.

'That was it,' Angelica said tonelessly.

'And you?'

She looked at him, outraged. '*No.* I would never be unfaithful.' Even while married to Aldo, the thought of another man…other than Leo…had been anathema. Angelica had frozen over inside. Until now.

'Aldo didn't corrupt you completely, then.'

Angelica clamped her mouth shut, afraid of what might come out.

Leo said, 'I would never be unfaithful within a marriage, even this one. Why would I? When all I want is standing right in front of me. There's not one woman back at that event who I would look at twice.'

Angelica had a flashback to Leo appearing in the doorway of the bathroom and telling her it was a mistake. 'It's not happening. I won't be some plaything for your cruel amusement.'

'I wasn't trying to be cruel.'

Angelica forced herself to meet his eye. 'It didn't feel that way.'

'I'm sorry.'

Angelica shook her head. 'There's too much history between us.'

'I agree. And maybe the only way to deal with it is to acknowledge it. Acknowledge that it's still in our present.'

'Because you engineered this whole situation.'

'I would have come for you,' Leo said in a low fervent voice, making Angelica's skin tighten. 'I never stopped thinking about you.'

She swallowed. 'You mean, wanting me to be punished.'

He shrugged minutely. 'Yes, I can't deny that…but since we've been together again, it's becoming less about that and more about…*this*.'

Angelica couldn't even formulate a word in response because Leo had moved closer and snaked a hand around the back of her neck, under her hair, and was tugging her towards him with no force. She was moving towards him willingly in spite of everything she'd just said and as soon as she realised that she dug her heels in.

'Leo…' Her voice sounded thready and weak.

'Yes, Angel…'

'I thought I told you—'

'Not to call you that, yes…'

But clearly he was unrepentant. He said, 'What will it take?'

Angelica's head felt fuzzy. 'Take for what?'

'To show you that you can trust me.'

'I…' She trailed off. Angelica knew in her heart of hearts that she did trust Leo. With this at least. He wouldn't do to her again what he'd done last night. And, in a way, she could see that if she had come to her senses, she might have had a similar reaction.

Then Leo said, 'How about if I…let you tie me up?'

CHAPTER SEVEN

A FLASH OF heat went straight to Angelica's core at the audacious suggestion. To have Leo at her mercy, begging and pleading. She could walk away and leave him there...get her own back. But of course she wouldn't have the nerve to do such a thing. Wouldn't want to.

'You'd let me do that?'

A flicker of uncertainty crossed his face and then it was gone. He nodded. A little devil inside Angelica made her say, 'OK, then.'

She stepped back and dislodged his hand and put out her hand. He looked at it for a moment and then put his hand in hers. As Angelica led him to the bedroom, her insides swooping and fizzing, she felt some measure of control for the first time in a long time.

In the bedroom Angelica let go of Leo's hand and turned to face him. Feeling bold, she said, 'Take your clothes off.'

He arched a brow. 'Please?'

'Please.'

Angelica wasn't sure if Leo would even comply. Maybe he'd come to his senses again and tell her to get out. But no, his fingers went to his bow tie and undid it, pulling it free and letting it drop to the ground.

Then he was undoing his shirt, button by button. Had time slowed down? Stopped even? It felt like that to Angelica. She couldn't take her eyes off his long fingers, the chest he was revealing, inch by muscled inch. The smattering of hair. The defined pectorals and then down, to the ridged abdominals.

His shirt was open and he pulled it off completely. It fell to the floor. Then his hands were on his belt. He opened it and then the top button. The zip. Angelica could see the bulge pressing against the material. *Good.* He wasn't as cool as he looked.

Her breaths were coming short and shallow. She had to focus and suck more air in. His hands were on the sides of his trousers now and with one graceful movement he pushed them down, taking his underwear with them.

He stepped out of the pile of clothes at his feet. He was naked. Gloriously, unashamedly, naked. Tall, proud. Virile. Angelica's gaze travelled over his form, relearning his body. Taking in that scar. The narrow hips. The hair at his groin, his erection. Long and heavy. Potent.

Muscled thighs. He was more ripped than she remembered him being. More densely muscled.

'Where do you want me?'

Angelica looked up, her mouth dry. He was really just letting her order him around? It was heady, this feeling of power. Although she knew if he touched her any illusion of power would be gone in an instant.

'On the bed, on your back.'

Leo went over to the bed, skin gleaming, muscles bunching and moving. He lay down on his back, one arm above his head. He said, 'You should probably get protection from the bathroom now.'

Angelica kicked off the shoes and went into the bathroom, finding the box of protective sheaths. She avoided looking at herself in the mirror. She could feel the heat in her cheeks. She took two foil packages out of the box and got even hotter.

She went back into the bedroom and saw the bow tie on the ground. She picked it up, not thinking too much about what she was doing because if she did she'd lose her nerve. She put the protection down on the bedside table, noting that Leo glanced at it but without looking at his expression. She knelt on the bed beside him and said, 'Give me one hand.'

He lifted the hand above his head and held it out. He was even more intimidating up close, and definitely far more muscled than he had been. *Prison.* Her heart spasmed. She ignored it and took his hand, wrapping the bow tie around his wrist and tying a knot, then she said, 'Your other hand.'

He dutifully held the other one out and in seconds she'd tied his wrists together securely. There was nothing else to tie them to, the headboard was solid wood.

He asked, 'Where did you learn to do that?'

'My father taught me. It's a sailor's knot.' She didn't want to think of her father now and the chain of violence that had ripped her family apart.

'I'm feeling a little undressed.'

Angelica looked at Leo. Her slicked-back hair was no longer slicked back, it was falling around her face. She got off the bed and in one fluid move—because the dress was made of jersey material—she pulled it up and off.

Now she wore only underwear. She reached behind her and undid the bra. She'd always had bigger proportions than the other models—breasts, hips—and had made something of a name for herself as *sexy*, which had come at a time when she was still figuring herself out.

It was only when she'd met this man that the moniker had made any kind of sense and she'd felt it. And the way he was looking at her now, she could see his eyes burning and his hands in fists, tied together.

She tucked her fingers into her lacy underpants and pulled them down, stepping out. She was naked. She could feel her nipples pulling into hard, tight points. Her breasts felt heavy.

'Come here, Angel, I need to touch you.'

She didn't have the wherewithal to tell him not to use that name. The truth was she liked it. She'd missed it. She walked to the bed and climbed on, and knelt before Leo.

He came up before her, on his knees too, and they faced each other for a moment. It felt, absurdly, almost spiritual. Then he lifted his bound hands and cupped her face and leant towards her and put his mouth on hers and then they were tumbling down onto the bed and all Angelica was aware of was the drugging, drowning sensation of losing herself in Leo's kiss.

Their bodies were pressed togther, her softness against his harder planes. He put a thigh between her legs and the centre of her body hummed in response.

Leo was on his back and Angelica was draped over him. The fact that his hands were bound meant his movements were curtailed, but as much as she wanted his hands everywhere, she was also enjoying his obvious frustration, eyes glittering hotly.

He said roughly, 'Come on top of me, Angel. I won't last long… I need you now.'

She needed him too. Her body was aching to know him again. First, she reached for the protection and then, with barely steady hands, she took it out of the package and knelt before him again. Carefully, slowly, she rolled the protective sheath onto Leo's body, aware of his hitched breathing, the hiss between his teeth. The way his hips jerked.

And then, she came over him, legs either side of his hips. She lifted herself, and, reaching behind her, she took him in her hand and guided him to where she was on fire. He breached her entrance and Angelica closed her eyes for a moment, hovering in that place between being full, and not.

And then, when she was ready, she slowly sank down, taking Leo's body inside hers. It was all at once exquisitely familiar and new.

'*Dio*, Angel…'

She looked down and, through her own hazy vision, she could see the perspiration on Leo's brow and the almost fevered look in his eyes. She couldn't speak, could hardly breathe at the sensation. It had been so long.

Slowly, she started to move. She put her hands on his chest and she could feel his heart pumping, in time with hers. Getting faster.

'Yes, like that.'

It was a primal dance, and Angelica was swept along, at Leo's urgings. He lifted his bound hands and squeezed the flesh of her breasts, one after the other, pinching the peaks. She leant over him, so he could put his mouth around her and suck the pebbled flesh. Her hair fell around them in a curtain, and then, when she needed more, she sat back up again and Leo spanned his hands across her midriff, to her waist, holding her as best he could.

Their movements got more frantic as the climax approached and it took Angelica by surprise, mocking her belief that she had any kind of control, as she felt her body hover on the edge for a second before falling down and down into a pulsating, clasping ocean of pleasure.

Leo wasn't far behind her, hips thrusting up, his body tight and taut as he too went over the edge and she could feel the release run through his muscles. She thought she'd have his finger marks in her flesh like a brand as he sought to hold her still. And then, with a hoarse cry, he sank back and all that could be heard was their ragged breathing. Their skin was damp.

Angelica couldn't do anything else but slump over Leo and she felt him bring his bound hands and arms over her head and body to hold her against him.

She closed her eyes and fell into a dreamless place of peace and satisfaction, so profound, she knew even then that it was far too dangerous for her to analyse, so she didn't.

At some point, Angelica woke again and found she was on her side, facing Leo. His eyes were open. Their bodies were close together, close enough for her to feel him stir against her. And then she realised that his hands were no longer bound because one hand was rubbing up and down her back and the other was between them.

'How did you untie the knot?'

'I never told you but my grandfather was a fisherman and taught me how to undo all the sailor's knots.'

'You knew the whole time.'

He nodded, a smile ghosting across his mouth. Like this, Angelica could almost fool herself into believing the past three years hadn't happened. That they hadn't broken up. That maybe, outside that window was Venice and the Grand Canal and if they could go back in time and she didn't tell him she loved him then maybe—

He put a finger over her mouth. It still felt tender after his kisses.

'Stop.'

She scowled. He'd always been able to see her brain whirring. She put her tongue out and tasted his finger before putting her mouth around it and biting gently.

His body hardened against her belly and the air between them became thick with desire and urgency.

This time, with no restraints and no need to fear that he would stop and reject her, Angelica gave herself over to the lavish attentions of Leo, his hands running all over body as if he needed to relearn every dip and hollow.

When he came over her, she widened her legs and as he entered her she sucked in a breath, her body still a little sensitive after the first time.

He stopped. 'OK?'

She nodded. 'Fine, keep going.' She put her hands on his buttocks and squeezed and Leo pushed all the way in, before moving out again, and taking them on a slow and sensual dance, building to a climax that ripped through their bodies simultaneously, wringing pleasure out of every nerve ending and cell in their bodies, leaving them clinging to one another as if they'd both been buffeted by a massive storm.

The next morning, Leo felt disorientated. It was light outside. He was used to waking at dawn. He was on his own in the bed and the only signs that he hadn't hallucinated the previous hours were the discarded foil packets of protection they'd used, and the bow tie, lying on the pillow beside him.

His body felt…replete in a way it hadn't for a long time. Sated. At ease. The constant state of adrenalin that had stayed with him even since his release from prison had also diminished.

He closed his eyes for a moment and his brain was filled with images. Angelica above him, astride him, her sleek body taking him in with such exquisite slowness that he'd almost spilled then and there.

Her perfect breasts, and those pebbled nipples. Dark. Sweet and sharp against his tongue. The silky hot clasp of her body around his. He frowned and opened his eyes. She'd felt...almost like she had the first time he'd slept with her. *She'd been a virgin.*

But she'd been married since then. With Aldo for three years. *No.* He didn't want to go there. Anyway, she'd revealed that Aldo had been unfaithful so maybe she'd shut him out of the bedroom. Maybe that had been the cause of the discontent, but the thought of Angelica being so humiliated and badly treated—possibly emotionally upset because of Aldo's infidelity—drove Leo up and out of bed and into the shower.

Where was she? Before, when they'd been together, she'd always surprised Leo by not wanting to wake up together. He'd been used to her leaving early or, if they'd been in her small apartment, she'd be up and making breakfast, busy.

It had only been after a couple of weeks that she'd confided that she'd been aware that his relationships never lasted longer than a night or two, so she hadn't wanted to seem clingy.

It was Leo who had encouraged her to stay in bed... when he'd never done that before, with a woman. While in prison, that had tortured him, the idea that she'd played him so well, but now...

After washing, he pulled on clothes and went out into the main part of the apartment suite. Angelica was having breakfast, dressed, in jeans and a long-sleeved cashmere top. Hair damp and tied up loosely. Face fresh. No make-up. She looked at him and a little flush came into her cheeks. Leo felt slightly off-centre, as if she was ahead of him on something. Knew something he didn't.

'Hi, sorry, I forgot that I have to go to Madrid today for work, for a couple of days. I meant to tell you last night but then…' She trailed off, her cheeks going pinker.

'You could have told me at the party, or before.'

She looked down at the croissant she was cutting open, and shrugged minutely. 'To be honest, it went out of my head.'

Leo went over and sat down opposite her and helped himself to some coffee. She was still avoiding his eye. Something about that…some sense that something else was going on here made him say, 'I'll come with you.'

Now her head came up and she looked at him, the colour fading from her cheeks. 'Why would you do that? You have work here.'

She was up to something. He felt exposed. Had last night just been a diversionary tactic? 'It's no problem,' he said easily. 'I have some contacts in Madrid that I could use meeting again, face to face, to asssure them that all is well. We can use my plane.'

'My agent has organised transport.'

Leo smiled but he felt grim. 'I'm sure it can be cancelled.'

Angelica picked up her coffee cup and Leo noticed the slightest tremor in her hand. She said, 'OK, if you're sure you don't mind changing your plans.'

'Oh, I don't mind at all,' he said, calling himself all sorts of a fool for not suspecting that she had been up to something all along. *You seduced her,* pointed out a little voice. Perhaps, he had to concede, but after living with Aldo for three years maybe she'd become as adept as he had been in the art of making you believe you were the one in control and making decisions. If he'd learned one thing in the last three years it was not to let himself ever be taken for a fool again.

As the plane descended into Madrid, Angelica tried to keep her expression neutral. She couldn't believe that she'd let Leo distract her so much that she'd almost forgotten that she was coming here. And that she might have a chance to see her mother and brother.

Surely, she could carve out an hour somewhere to meet them, before or after the job she'd agreed to do. If Leo was having meetings it should be easy. And she would finally, *finally*, see them again and be able to hug them and touch them and tell them everything.

She'd had to be so careful, and she hadn't been able to go into the full details of her marriage with Leo, saying only that she was OK and that she'd explain when she could.

'Penny for them?'

Angelica looked at Leo and realised she was smiling to herself. She composed herself and mentally crossed her fingers, saying, 'The photographer I'm working with, she's one of my best friends, we started out together in the business, I'm looking forward to seeing her...' That wasn't a lie. It just wasn't the reason why she'd engineered to come here.

'What's her name?' Leo asked sharply. Angelica's insides sank. He sensed something was up.

'Natalja Jordan Segal. She's just returned to work from maternity leave. She had her third baby over a year ago.'

The thought that, even after last night, Leo still didn't trust her made something inside her shrivel up. And made her more determined than ever to connect with her family. She was glad now that she'd woken before him this morning and had managed to get her bearings. She needed them.

She said, 'A car is meeting me at the airport to take me straight to the shoot. I'll be back at the hotel early this evening.'

'I've lined up a dinner with some business associates. I'd like it if you were there too.'

Angelica looked at Leo. 'OK, sure.'

When the plane landed, Angelica was directed to the sleek SUV waiting for her, and she tried not to let Leo see how excited and also trepidatious she felt to be in the same city as her family. She'd never have dared to come anywhere near them while married to Aldo.

'See you this evening, Angel.'

She glanced back at Leo just before she got into the car. He was wearing a dark blue suit and shades. Every inch the powerful titan. All at once achingly familiar, and almost like a stranger that she was still getting to know. *To trust.*

He hadn't been a stranger last night. In a bid to avoid thinking about the significance of what had happened and wondering if it would happen again, Angelica said, 'See you later,' and got into the car.

That evening, Leo's car pulled to a stop outside a warehouse on the outskirts of the city. He'd got a text from Angelica during the afternoon, *Hi, I'm really sorry but we're going to have to go late here, I won't make the dinner.*

After finishing the business dinner Leo had decided to come and pick Angelica up from the shoot. He went into the cavernous space where there seemed to be hundreds of people milling about.

Something eased inside him to see she'd been telling the truth. Maybe he was just being paranoid?

And then he saw her and stopped. She was standing against a black backdrop in a gold dress made of some shimmery material that looked as if it had been poured directly onto her body, lovingly outlining every curve, dip and hollow.

For a second, Leo had to battle with a blast of pure lust so strong that he wanted to stride in there, yell at everyone to stop looking at her and pick her up and take her away.

He took a breath. She looked smaller and somehow more fragile against the massive backdrop and with everyone scurrying around her. He noticed that she looked faintly weary and thought of how little sleep they'd got the previous night. His body tightened at the memory. And in anticipation of re-enacting it. It was just lust. Physical desire. Unfinished business.

Suddenly everyone seemed to snap to attention. A couple of people were touching up Angelica's make-up and hair, and the dress. A slim woman with blonde hair tied up in a messy bun had a camera in her hands and was directing proceedings. That had to be Angelica's friend.

And then, after about another half an hour, someone called out, 'OK, guys, thanks for a great day, that's a wrap.'

There was a smattering of clapping and laughter. Angelica was smiling and hugging the photographer. And then over the woman's shoulder she saw Leo and her eyes widened and the smile faded. He felt it like a punch to the gut. She wasn't happy to see him.

When she'd extricated herself from her friend's embrace, she came towards him, holding the dress up with one hand. Her hair was styled in glossy Hollywood waves. She stood before him. 'You didn't have to come all the way here.'

'It was no problem. Dinner finished early.'

'How did it go?'

'Fine. Constructive.'

'I'll just get changed and get my things.'

Leo nodded, and watched her walk away. Someone came up to her with what looked like her handbag and Angelica smiled at them in a way that he remembered from before. She'd smiled easily a lot, and she'd been sweet. Or, she'd certainly faked it well.

Leo ignored the voice calling him churlish. What

else was he supposed to think when she'd gone and betrayed him so heinously?

But then another memory came back—he'd gone to one of her shoots while they'd been together and when a photographer had bawled out a young assistant, Angelica had gone over and had words, forcing the photographer to apologise to the tearful assistant.

Afterwards he'd told her what he'd seen and she'd said, 'I don't like people treating others badly. There's no need for it.'

He'd been impressed by her kindness. It was a rarity in the circles he moved in.

He lost Angelica momentarily in the crowd of people and searched her out, finding her eventually in that gold dress. She was standing on the other side of the space, head bent, looking at her phone. Fingers flying over the screen. Texting someone.

A dark weight slid into his gut. His instinct had been right all along.

Almost without thinking, Leo found that he was moving towards her. Until he was standing right beside her. She was oblivious. There was a small smile playing around her mouth, a secret smile. Like on the plane earlier. He went cold inside.

Acting on an impulse driven by something hot and red, Leo reached out and plucked the phone from Angelica's hands. Her head jerked up and she saw him and her phone in his hand and went white.

Leo looked down and scanned the text quickly, reading: I know, mi amor, I can't wait to see you too, if I can get away I will, I'll be in touch...

Like lightning, she had snatched the phone back and clutched it to her chest. There were two spots of pink high in her cheeks. 'How dare you?'

The thing uppermost in Leo's head was the familiar acrid sense of betrayal. Even more acute after last night. *You can tie me up.* The exposure was excoriating.

He bit out, 'You can tell your lover that you'll be free to meet him after all.'

But she was shaking her head. 'It's not like that... like you think.' She had a stricken look on her face, reminding him of that morning when she'd told him she loved him and he'd sent her away, out of his sight, before she could annihilate him.

She'd annihilated him anyway. He was done. He'd been weak to pursue revenge like this. She'd all but made him a laughing stock over the past week—had it only been a week? It felt longer. He was a fool.

He turned away but she put a hand on his arm. 'Leo. Stop. Wait.'

Against every self-preserving instinct inside him, urging him to keep walking all the way out of this studio, until she was far behind him, he stopped. She came around him to stand in front of him and even in the midst of his recrimination she was exquisite. He knew in that moment that if he never looked at another woman again, he wouldn't care. Damn her.

'Angelica—'

She put up a hand. 'I'm not texting a lover.'

'Then who are you texting?' How was she going to weasel her way out of this? And also, why wasn't she just standing aside with a triumphant smile on her face, watching him walk away? Asking for a divorce? *Because she wants more. She's up to something.*

He saw her swallow. She looked nervous. Looking at him as if she wanted to look all the way into the deepest part of him. Losing patience, Leo was about to look away when she said, 'It's my brother. I'm texting my brother, Paolo.'

The words hung between them. Leo couldn't fully compute them. A brother. 'You never mentioned a brother before.'

'I couldn't. It wasn't safe.'

What on earth was she up to now? As if hearing his thoughts she shook her head. 'Just...please give me a chance to explain. I need to change out of this dress. Security are waiting for it because it's haute couture. Will you wait for me?'

Leo didn't know which way was up right now. She'd blindsided him. Much as she had when he'd seen pictures in the paper of her and Aldo.

'Please, just wait, OK?'

Angelica was changed back into her own clothes, jeans and the cashmere top. Make-up scrubbed off. Hair pulled back. She looked pale in the mirror. She hesitated before leaving the dressing room. She wasn't even sure if Leo was still outside. He might be gone. He might feel that whatever she was about to tell him was just one more provocation too far.

The intimacy of last night felt like aeons ago. Two steps forward and ten steps back.

Was she really going to reveal her family to him? *You just have,* pointed out a voice.

Yes. She had to tell him. She owed him this. The past week had worn away at her defences as she'd seen a man who had been betrayed heinously pick up the pieces of his life and start to rebuild it, brick by brick, with a cool, determined pragmatism.

She had to trust that he wouldn't use the information to threaten them, or her. *He wouldn't.* Somehow she knew that now. He had integrity. He wasn't Aldo. He hadn't changed in that respect.

She collected her bag and went outside where crew were packing up. At first she couldn't see him but then she did, and felt a spurt of relief. His tall, broad-shouldered figure was silhouetted in the opening to the studio. Back to her, hands in his pockets.

Her heart tripped and her pulse quickened. Damn him. As if sensing her, he turned around. She walked over, aware of her skin prickling.

His face was expressionless but he put out a hand for her bag, and just that small courtesy made her feel as though she was doing the right thing.

His car was waiting and he opened the back door to let her get in, before getting in on the other side. No words were exchanged. Angelica could feel the tension thrumming between them.

When they pulled up outside a Madrid hotel they got out. The concierge greeted Leo effusively. Angelica barely took in the sumptuous furnishings and hushed exclusivity. She just followed Leo. The elevator journey up to the suite was made in silence.

Their suite was at the end of a plushly carpeted hall and Leo opened the door, allowing Angelica to precede him. The suite was gorgeously lavish and luxurious. French doors led out to a terrace and she opened them, needing air.

The sun had set and Madrid glittered like a bauble spread out below. The air was mild. Still. An almost full moon hung in the sky. She hoped it wasn't a bad sign.

'Angelica.'

Angelica. Less than twenty-four hours ago it had been *Angel*. She forced herself to turn away from the view to face Leo. He was standing with hands on his hips. His face was no longer expressionless, it was grim. He'd taken off his tie and jacket.

Without preamble she said simply, 'I don't have a lover. I have a mother and brother who I helped get out of Italy to protect them and give them new lives.'

CHAPTER EIGHT

LEO MUST HAVE just been looking at her stupidly for a long moment because as he watched she went and fished her phone out of her bag and then she was holding it out to him. He looked down and saw an elegant middle-aged woman with dark hair going a little grey, and a young man, tall and skinny.

They were unmistakably related to Angelica. They all shared the dark hair, amazing bone structure and unusual eyes. They were smiling and the young man had his arm around his mother.

'I haven't seen them in four years.'

Leo looked at Angelica, still reeling. He handed back her phone. 'Why did you never tell me about them?'

'I couldn't. I was told to tell no one.'

'By who?'

'The charity who helped me get them out.' She put down her phone and paced away from Leo. He wanted to grab her arm and pull her back. There was a tightness building inside him.

She turned around. 'After my father was killed—'

'I just assumed you had no other family.'

She nodded. 'I know, and I didn't correct you.' She went on, 'After he was killed, Paolo was young, vulnerable, angry with the Mafia. And there was always a chance they could come and kill him and my mother too even though my father had been very peripheral to the gangs. It hadn't stopped them killing him. I was afraid Paolo would do something reckless to demonstrate his anger.'

'Where were you?'

'I was already gone, modelling. I was eighteen. I was terrified that Paolo would get caught up in the violence. Mama was, too. Then I read about the charity that does work getting people out...most people don't have the money to leave Italy and so they're still in danger, but I had enough to send them further. Mama changed their name to her grandmother's maiden name. Paolo found it difficult to adapt at first, understandably...but now he's graduating from university with a degree in law and they've both built new lives for themselves, away from the grief and violence.'

Leo could hear the pride and emotion in her voice. But this was...huge. Acting on instinct and needing a moment to get his wits together, he went over to the drinks cabinet and poured himself a slug of whiskey.

Remembering himself at the last moment, he looked back at Angelica. She was pale, eyes huge, and it caught at him deep inside. He tensed against it. 'Would you like anything?'

She shook her head. 'No, thank you... Leo... I—'

He held up the glass, stopping her. 'Just give me a second...'

He put the glass down and ran a hand through his hair. He felt as if he were coming undone. He also felt...a kind of gut-punch sensation to acknowledge that she hadn't told him before.

'Why didn't you tell me? Before?'

Her throat moved as she swallowed. 'Because I was told to trust no one for at least the first year of their relocation. I wasn't allowed to see them. You know the world we came from. You know how anyone affiliated with people they've killed are at risk. It was dangerous. Paolo was just starting to settle down... I couldn't jeopardise their safety...'

'You didn't trust me.'

'I was going to tell you. The day...the day that we broke up.'

The day she'd said: *I love you, Leo.* He recalled all too easily the terror that had entered his veins at the thought of what those words meant. Destruction. Devastation. He'd wondered how had he let it get that far?

But, if he was being entirely honest, those words hadn't just evoked terror, they'd evoked something even worse. *Hope.* The very tiny fledgling seed of something he hadn't ever dared to imagine because it could never happen. In case it was taken away from him again.

But *she hadn't meant it*. Or, had she? Leo didn't know any more. He couldn't think of that now.

'Did Aldo know?'

She nodded slowly. Leo's jaw tightened and fire

filled his veins. He hadn't known but that snake had. Of course, just more evidence of her collusion.

'But not like you think.'

Leo almost didn't hear her through the roaring in his head. He frowned. 'What do you mean?'

'I never told him. He found out…he must have done some digging… Not long after you and I broke up, he came to my apartment in Rome.'

Now Angelica looked green. She said, 'Actually, maybe I will have a small drink.'

Leo poured her a measure of whiskey and brought it over. She took it and threw it back, wincing. It took some of the green from her expression though. She handed it back to him and he put the glass down, and took a step back, folding his arms. 'Go on.'

She started to pace again and Leo had to force his gaze up and not let it move down over her body. Even now she had the power to distract him.

'He came and I couldn't understand why he was there because I barely knew him…only through meeting him at events with you.' She stopped and looked at Leo and her eyes were very green. 'You have to believe me, there was nothing going on.'

Leo said nothing. She went on, 'He told me that he had information about me, and he showed me pictures of my mother and brother going about their business. I couldn't believe it…' She was shaking her head, and Leo could see the memory of that terror on her face.

If she was acting then she deserved an Oscar, and, uncomfortably, he had to admit that he didn't think she was acting. After everything that had happened, he could fully accept Aldo was capable of such a thing.

'Aldo told me that unless I did as he asked, he would instruct people to hurt…and do possibly worse, to my mother and brother.'

Leo had always known that Aldo had kept ties with some of the people from his past connected with the Mafia but he'd never appreciated how much until everything had blown up.

'What did he ask?' But he knew. And now Leo felt sick. Because if what Angelica was about to say—

'He told me I had to marry him.'

Just as *he'd* told her she had to marry him. For a moment Leo thought he would be sick but it passed. He felt clammy. Made her say it again. 'He, what?'

'Told me I had to marry him, or he would go after my mother and brother.'

'So you…him…'

She shook her head and he saw her eyes burn. 'I despised that man. He was odious.'

An awful image sprang into Leo's head. 'Did he force you—?'

Angelica put up a hand. 'No.' She stopped, swallowed. 'He wanted to…he tried—' She shuddered visibly before continuing, 'But he couldn't…do it. I think it was the guilt at what he was doing to you, and me. He obviously looked at me and saw you. Then because I'd witnessed him not being able to…perform, he didn't come near me again in any kind of intimate way. He got angry, blamed you. He blamed you for everything. He hated you so much. He was so envious of your success because he knew it wasn't really down to him. Throughout the marriage he slept with multitudes of women, and some men. He wasn't above paying for their services.'

Leo obeyed an instinct too strong to ignore—he closed the distance between him and Angelica and put his hands on her arms. 'But he didn't touch you... Did he ever strike you? Take his anger out on you?'

She shook her head. Her hair had been tied back but it was loose now, falling over her shoulders. 'No,' she whispered. 'I think once he couldn't...perform, every time he looked at me I was like a symbol of his guilty conscience or something. He just used me for public appearances and I made sure to work as much as possible. But he didn't mind that because he loved being married to a model, someone in the public eye.'

The relief rushing through Leo to know that Aldo hadn't touched her made him almost feel weak. He took his hands down. Angelica wrapped her arms around herself. Leo went and closed the French doors, and pulled a throw from the back of a chair and put it around Angelica's shoulders. 'You're cold.'

'I'm OK, really.' But she sat down. Leo got another small slug of whiskey and brought one over for her and one for him. She held it in her hands. This was huge... what she was telling him. Almost too huge for him to interpret because, frankly, it was horrific.

But one thing was clear and he had to address it. He put down his glass and sat down on a chair opposite her. 'Angelica...'

She looked at him and suddenly he could see the

toll of the last four, three, years on her face. In a weariness. He saw it because he felt it too.

I love you, Leo. He pushed the memory down because if everything she was saying now was true... then that also...had been true.

'If you had never met me, you wouldn't have met Aldo and he wouldn't have come into your life like a poison, threatening your family, forcing you into an impossible situation.'

She looked at him. 'You believe me.'

'Yes,' he said simply. It was all too awfully believable. But he couldn't untangle everything now. There were more important concerns. 'Where are your mother and brother now?'

Angelica's eyes shimmered. 'They're here, in Madrid, that's why I jumped at the opportunity to come here for work. They're in a suburb just outside the city. Now that Aldo is dead, they're finally safe.'

Anger surged inside Leo. 'They should have always been safe.'

'That wasn't your fault. Aldo was toxic, more toxic than you ever could have imagined. There's no point looking back.'

Leo felt cold inside. 'We were both in a prison of Aldo's making. I'm so sorry.'

He thought back to the day of the funeral, all but dragging her to a church to force her to marry him. He shook his head, 'How could you let me treat you the way I did?'

She shrugged a little. 'I didn't know who you were any more, who you'd become. The Leo I knew would never have threatened another person but you'd been in prison. I had no idea how that might have affected you. I knew you must believe I'd betrayed you. And after Aldo using my family to blackmail me, I was hardly going to trust someone who clearly hated me.'

He shook his head. 'I never hated you, Angel... I was angry, betrayed...but what I feel for you is not hate.'

It certainly isn't love, either. Not that she wanted love, she told herself hastily. Been there, got the heartbreak T-shirt. What they had now was the remnants of the chemistry that had first brought them together. And maybe now that was gone too...not for her, she could still feel every part of her humming just to be near Leo, but maybe this would have pushed him too far.

Even so, Angelica felt as if a weight had been lifted from her entire body. This was the first time she'd ever willingly told anyone about her family.

There was something very fragile between them now. As if scaffolding had been ripped away, leaving them exposed, with nothing to hide behind. She felt vulnerable. Now he knew...and she had to be sure.

'You won't use this information to...threaten them or hurt them, will you?'

Leo looked at her and numerous expressions crossed his face, disbelief, horror, disgust and then anger. He stood up. '*No*, how could you think such a thing?'

'Because I've lived with that fear for the last three years.'

Leo paced back and forth. He stopped and looked at

her and his face was stark. He said in a slightly more modulated tone, 'Of course I wouldn't do anything to harm them, or use them against you.'

Angelica sucked in a breath. 'Thank you.'

Leo said, 'If Aldo had touched you…'

Angelica stood up. 'But he didn't. He couldn't. He was a coward.' But she understood what Leo meant. If Aldo had really wanted to violate her, she wouldn't have been able to stop him.

'That's where you were going to the day of the funeral? To see your mother and brother?'

Angelica nodded. 'Yes, I was coming here.'

Leo looked at his watch. 'You're here now, you shouldn't have to wait any longer.'

Angelica's heart beat fast, her eyes widened. 'You mean it? Now?'

Leo nodded. 'I'll get my driver ready.'

Angelica put a hand to her mouth, afraid the emotion would tumble out, and then she acted on impulse, crossing the space to Leo and throwing her arms around his neck. For a moment he did nothing, as if stunned, and then his arms came around her and they were welded together, torso to torso, hip to hip. 'Thank you,' Angelica said brokenly and pressed a kiss to his neck. His scent flooded her nostrils and by the time she pulled away she was shaking.

'I'll just…freshen up and let them know.'

She left the room before she threw herself back into Leo's arms and got ready in a daze, not even sure if she wasn't dreaming. She was afraid to pinch herself and wake up.

She pulled on some fresh clothes, trousers and a shirt, and got a soft leather jacket out of the wardrobe. She pulled on flat boots. She did her best with some make-up to try and look less…emotionally wrung out.

When she went back into the main part of the suite, Leo was on the phone. He terminated his conversation, eyes raking over her. He said, 'My driver is waiting downstairs. He'll take you wherever you need to go.'

Angelica felt as if she were on a precipice. What happened now? After this? Where did this leave them?

He said, 'Maybe we can talk after you've spent some time with them.'

Angelica nodded. 'Of course.' She went to make her way to the door but Leo didn't move. She looked back. 'Aren't you coming?' It hadn't even occurred to her that he might not be with her and she didn't want to analyse the significance of that now.

'You want me to come?'

'I'd like you to meet them.'

'But you haven't seen them in years.'

'I know…it's OK.' She felt exposed now. 'That is unless you have something else to do, it's—'

But he was grabbing his jacket and saying, 'No, let's go.'

The journey to the suburbs seemed both endless and quicker than a nanosecond. They pulled into a quiet street with very ordinary apartment blocks. Leo could feel Angelica almost vibrating beside him. He had to to curb the urge to take her hand in his.

Everything had changed with this revelation. But they would discuss that. He could see a woman and a tall young man under a streetlight. Waiting outside a building. Angelica let out a sound and he looked over to see her hand over her mouth and tears falling freely from her eyes.

He instructed the driver to stop. The car had barely pulled in before she was out of the car and running straight into the arms of the woman and young man.

For a second, Leo stayed in the car, feeling a tightness in his chest, and expanding outwards. For years after his family had been killed in front of him, whenever he'd seen any kind of family unit, he'd experienced panic attacks. He hadn't had to see a psychologist to understand that he most likely had PTSD and saw danger and horror in a scenario that anyone else would see as totally benign.

But over time he'd learned to control his reaction. Except now, with Angelica lost in a tangle of arms and heads, he felt close to one again, for the first time in a long time.

He forced himself out of the car and the young man looked at him over Angelica's shoulder. He said something to her and she extricated herself from the tangle of arms. Leo saw the tears on her mother's face.

Angelica beckoned him to come over and he forced himself forward even though an instinct was telling him to run. She introduced them to him and he shook hands, aware of their curious looks, especially Angelica's younger brother, who stood beside her protectively.

'Can I have a word?' Leo asked pointedly.

She nodded and moved away from her mother and brother. Leo said, 'You need some time with them. Take as long as you need. I'll be in Madrid for two more days. We should talk before I leave.'

She looked at him, eyes wide, glistening, full of emotion. 'I... OK, yes, I'll be in touch. Thank you, Leo, for letting me come to them.'

He shook his head. He owed her. So much. This was the start. They'd both been victims of Aldo's perverse toxic jealousy. Perhaps her, even more so.

Leo gave a little salute to her mother and brother and then went back to the car, instructing the driver to take him back to the hotel. He didn't look behind him to see the family unit again. He didn't need to. It was ingrained on his brain, and it tugged far too dangerously on the tiny little seed of hope he'd felt when Angelica had told him she loved him, before he'd crushed it three years ago.

If anything, this only reinforced his determination to never put himself in that danger again. It was time to let Angelica go. For good this time.

Two days later

Angelica returned to the hotel in the centre of Madrid. For the first time in years, she finally felt at peace. Whole again. The past forty-eight hours with her mother and brother had healed her. And the fact that she could see them any time...still felt like a dream.

Her brother was doing so well, getting an internship

with a big legal firm and moving in with a girlfriend. Her mother was embarking on a very slow and tentative relationship with a retired widowed man who she'd met at a local bookclub.

They were happy. Thriving. And so now it was just Angelica who needed to get on with *her* life. But she couldn't see past Leo. As she ascended in the elevator to the suite, she truly had no idea what to expect.

She stepped into the suite and heard Leo's deep voice before she saw him. Her skin prickled with awareness. The cacophony of voices and questions in her head stopped when she saw him standing at the open French doors with a phone lifted to his ear. Wearing a white shirt tucked into dark trousers. The plain clothes did nothing to disguise his powerful body. She could imagine him in a boxing ring. Maybe that was what he'd done in prison. Imagining her and Aldo as he'd taken lumps out of someone.

He'd told her he didn't hate her but she had a feeling that whatever he did feel for her most likely wasn't enough to sustain a marriage built on a need for revenge and rehabilitation. The need for revenge was gone and Angelica hadn't really done much to help Leo's image in public, apart from, as he'd said, diverting attention away from his rebuilding and rebranding of his business.

And then he turned around and saw her and her heart palpitated. *She still loved him.* No. *No!* She couldn't still love him. He'd crushed her love for him three years ago, ground it into dust. All she felt now was desire but that assertion stuck in her chest like a boulder, constricting and tight.

After he terminated his phone conversation he said, 'I wasn't sure if I would see you again.'

And he didn't seem to be too devastated by that prospect. Angelica pushed the vulnerability down. She lifted a hand where her rings sat. 'We're still married, in case you forgot.'

'We don't have to be. We can initiate divorce proceedings as soon as you like.'

Angelica spoke slowly. 'As soon as *I* like.'

He nodded. 'I forced you into this marriage, Angelica, seeking revenge. I did you a great disservice.'

Angelica. Her insides clutched. He looked so distant. Sounded so formal. 'You didn't know—you didn't have all the information.'

His mouth twisted. 'Because you were terrified I would threaten your family's safety if you told me.'

She swallowed. 'I think I knew, even then, that you wouldn't ever do anything like Aldo had…but it all happened so fast…and I did feel guilty. I knew you were innocent but I couldn't do anything to help you.'

'Because you were in a prison too.'

'Not like you.' Angelica shuddered when she thought of the scar on Leo's body. What he'd had to endure in that place.

'How are your family?'

Her tension dissipated. She couldn't help smiling. 'They're amazing. Thank you for letting me be with them.'

'You're free now to do whatever you want.'

'What does that mean?'

'I'm letting you go, Angel. I should never have come for you. I needed to punish someone...and Aldo was gone.'

Angel. There was the spark of something...she could cling onto. All she knew was that the thought of turning around and walking back out of the door and out of Leo's life was impossible. Even if he was actively trying to get rid of her.

Bluntly she asked, 'You said we had unfinished business. Do you still want me?'

Leo's cheeks flushed. 'Looking at you right now, I don't know if I can imagine a time when I won't want you.'

Angelica nearly sagged against the chair near her. She couldn't believe she'd had the nerve to ask that. He still wanted her. The relief was sharp and sweet.

She slipped off her jacket and let it and her bag drop into a chair. She walked towards Leo. His gaze narrowed. 'What are you doing?'

She stopped in front of him. 'We made an agreement, to marry and rehabilitate your image.'

'It was hardly an agreement. That's why I can't ask you to stay.'

'Do you want me to, though?'

His eyes flared golden. But he said, 'It's not about what I want.'

'Well, what about what *I* want?'

'What do you want?'

'You.' She couldn't believe she was being so forward but since she'd unburdened herself and seen her family again, she felt liberated.

'This isn't a good idea, Angel. We have too much history.'

'Precisely why we need to exorcise it. Aldo took three years of our lives and almost ruined your reputation and everything you built up. You deserve to have it all back.'

'And what about you?'

She felt emotional. 'I have my family and for now that's enough. I've used my work for the last three years as a buffer between me and a sadist, but I don't even know if I want to do that any more. I want something more meaningful.' *A family.* The words popped into her head and she had to push them away. That was not something Leo could give her, she'd known it subconsciously three years ago and he'd only confirmed it since then, but she knew she'd never be able to move on with someone else while this electric charge existed between them.

As if he couldn't help himself, Leo reached out and touched her jaw. 'So, what are you proposing?'

She moved a tiny bit closer. 'I can act the part of a dutiful, socially acceptable wife. Let me do that for you.'

'No more Lady Godiva moments?'

She shook her head and felt her face heat up. 'Not unless you specifically request it.'

'And?'

Her throat suddenly felt dry. This was the most forward she'd ever been in her life. 'And…while we both still want each other, why not let it burn itself out?'

He took a step back and said, 'Three years ago, you told me you loved me. Nothing has changed… I can't offer anything more.'

Angelica strove to look as nonchalant as possible. 'Three years ago I was naive. You were my first lover. I was infatuated.'

'I'm still your first and only lover,' Leo pointed out.

She flushed. She wasn't in love with him. She wasn't. 'And you won't be my last. I know that. I do want a family some day, Leo, and I know you don't want that, but that day is a long way off.'

He went a little pale. 'We both come from a past where family puts you and them in jeopardy. How can you risk that? You've seen it first hand—your own family have been used against you.'

'And they're the only thing that kept me going and sane through the past three years. If we lose hope in the future, then what's the point in anything?'

Angelica held her breath, waiting for Leo's answer. Eventually he said, 'Nothing has changed for me in that regard. If anything the last three years have only made me more determined not to subject loved ones to what you went through with your mother and brother.'

'I'm not asking you to change.' *Liar*.

The distance between them suddenly seemed like a chasm. Feeling a sense of defeat, Angelica said, 'Look, Leo, if you want to end this marriage now, then we go our separate ways for good. Maybe that's for the best...' She looked around for where she'd dropped her bag and jacket when her upper arm was taken in a firm grip.

She looked up and into Leo's face and the stark intent and hunger in his expression told her all she needed to know about what he thought of that idea. Her heart leapt.

'Why would I want to end this marriage when we haven't even had a honeymoon yet?'

Angelica blinked at him. She hadn't expected that. 'A honeymoon?'

He nodded and tugged her closer, until their bodies were touching. He cupped her jaw and his thumb rubbed her bottom lip. She wanted to flick out her tongue and taste him. Her knees felt weak.

'I can't think of two people who deserve a honeymoon break more, can you? After everything we've been through?'

A slow unfurling of heat made Angelica's insides tighten with anticipation. She shook her head. 'No.'

'Good, then how ready are you to leave right now?'

Angelica smiled and it felt good. She pushed aside the voices telling her she was playing with danger, courting Leo like this. He'd already hurt her once, he couldn't do it again. 'I'm ready.'

CHAPTER NINE

ANGELICA WAS IN HEAVEN. She'd never been so relaxed. The sun beat down but she was under the shade of an umbrella so it wasn't too intense. The lapping of waves against the shore came from nearby. The only other sounds were birds, circling high in the air. And insects in the lush vegetation that bordered the small, private beach.

The entire island, a little jewel in the Caribbean, was private. The only thing on the island was a luxurious and very exclusive resort, with dwellings so spread out that, since they'd arrived, Angelica had only caught glimpses of other people in the distance.

They had a beach villa. A vast open-plan space, with a private pool and this private section of beach. When they'd arrived the day before, Angelica had had a massage in the villa's spa room and her bones still felt like putty.

She'd lain down on the bed after her massage, while Leo had his massage, and had woken up this morning, still in the robe, after sleeping straight through.

She'd found Leo, bare-chested, wearing shorts, on the terrace having breakfast, which had been set up for them by staff. She'd felt shy, still not believing that he'd really spirited them away to this paradise for a honeymoon, even if it wasn't a real honeymon. It had suddenly felt like it.

She'd said, 'Sorry, I had no idea how tired I was.'

He'd smiled, and admitted, 'I fell into a coma too.' Then he'd held out an arm and said, 'Come here.'

Angelica had gone over and he'd pulled her into his lap. He'd looked at her for a long moment and then just said, 'Hi.'

Angelica had felt absurdly emotional. 'Hi.'

'How hungry are you?'

Sitting on his lap, his hard body under hers, all around her, she'd only been hungry for one thing. 'Not very.'

Needing no further encouragement, he'd lifted her effortlessly and brought her back inside to the bedroom. Within seconds they'd been naked and on the bed in a tangle of limbs, urgency in the air. When Leo had reached for protection, Angelica had stopped him, saying, 'I'm still on the pill... I didn't come off it during...the marriage. I was afraid to in case...' She'd trailed off, and winced inwardly when she'd seen Leo's expression darken.

But then he'd put the protection aside and said, 'I will make it up to you Angel. You shouldn't have ever had to endure that torture.'

She'd reached a hand up to his face and jaw. 'You don't owe me anything. It's over now, we're here, he's not. I never thought we'd be together again, like this.'

Leo hadn't said anything, he'd just joined their bodies in one cataclysmic thrust, stealing any more words from Angelica's mouth and any rational thoughts from her head.

Angelica heard the sounds of someone wading out of the water and lifted her head, shading her eyes with her hand. Leo was emerging from the sea and he took her breath away. Dark hair wet and flattened to his skull only drew the attention to the bone structure of his face.

In short swimming trunks that left little to the imagination, he was hewn from rock and steel. Every glorious inch bronzed and rippling. He was a sea god. A maruading pirate. And he was coming for her, it was in every taut line of his face and body.

'You should have come in, it's beautiful.'

'I'm enjoying the view.'

'Are you, now?'

She nodded. He reached down a hand and said, 'Time for a siesta?'

Angelica lifted up her hand and he grabbed it, pulling her up. Her skin was sandy. She felt young and carefree. As she'd felt when she'd first met Leo. Until he'd dumped her. She pushed aside the unwelcome dark shadow. No shadows here. She knew what this was. A diversion. An exorcism. A sexorcism.

'That sounds good.'

A wicked glint came into Leo's eye and before she knew what was happening, he'd ducked down and she was over his shoulder, one hand on her bottom, tapping it, and as he headed back towards the sea he said, 'A siesta is only earned after a little physical exercise.'

Angelica squealed as they hit the water and once they were out deep enough, Leo dunked her. She came up spluttering and laughing. 'You're so dead, Falzone.' She splashed him and he ducked under the water and pulled her under. They kissed, and their bodies intertwined as they rose lazily back to the surface, sucking in gulps of air.

She had her legs wrapped around Leo's hips and her arms around his neck. Mouths hovering mere centimetres apart.

A little breathlessly Leo said, 'I think that's enough exercise for now.'

Angelica rocked her hips against Leo's erection. 'I agree. I'm ready for my siesta.'

They swam back into shore and walked up the small beach, hand in hand, across the lush lawn and into the villa.

Dusk was falling over paradise a few hours later, as Leo looked out over the view. They'd spent the afternoon in bed and he hated to admit it but it hadn't felt like just sex. It had felt somehow deeper. As if they were coming back to each other. As if there'd just been some sort of a hiatus in their relationship, and not a violent schism.

He would never ordinarily choose to come to a place like this with a woman, a lover, because it would send all sorts of wrong signals.

And yet he hadn't hesitated to suggest it to Angelica. *Angel.* But this was no ordinary situation and it never had been with her, not even when they'd first been together. All the usual rules had gone out of the window. She'd been almost more independent than him.

He'd had no hint of her falling for him, which was why he'd got such a shock when she'd blurted it out. She'd said it was an infatuation. Maybe she was right. She'd been young. He had been her first lover. They were both older and bruised and battered after the last three years. If Angelica had been a romantic, she wouldn't be any more.

So, she was the perfect woman to bring to a place like this because they both knew this had no future, not once the chemistry had burnt itself out.

A noise from behind him made him turn around to see the staff completing setting the dinner table on the terrace. There was a buffet set up on a table nearby, groaning under the weight of different foods. Fish, salad, pitta bread, hummus, succulent meat on skewers.

And then Angel appeared looking like a vision. In a strapless long loose kaftan-style dress of a million different colours, her hair caught up in a loose bun. Even from here he could see the golden glow the sun had added to her skin. And he noticed too that she looked less…weary. Jaded. There had been a little frown etched between her eyebrows since they'd met again—*since you kidnapped her,* pointed out a voice. Leo's conscience prickled. He would make sure neither she, nor her family, would ever want for anything again.

What about when she has a family of her own?

asked another little voice. Well, then she wouldn't need his protection anymore. Leo's chest tightened at the thought of someone else having that privilege in her life. Angel would make an amazing mother.

He wouldn't be part of that scenario. Even just the thought of risking the same thing happening to Angel that had happened to his mother—gunned down in cold blood—was enough to have a familiar roiling sensation in his gut, and his breath becoming more shallow.

He focused on her now to divert his mind form the horror. She was gracious with the staff, smiling and gesticulating and thanking them for such a beautiful display of food. They beamed at her. He could empathise.

She saw him and walked over. Barefoot. Face free of make-up. No jewellery. Eyes very green. She'd never looked more beautiful. Leo focused on that to stem the rising tide of panic.

She said, 'Did you see the layout of food? It looks amazing. They've outdone themselves. Come on, I'm starving.' She caught his arm and led him back into the flickering light of candles dotted around the space and he allowed her to soothe the jagged edges inside him.

They filled up their plates and sat down. Angelica said, 'It's been so long since I've been able to just sit like this and eat good food.'

'Still not cooking for yourself?' Leo asked, unwittingly opening up the conversation to a memory of the past.

Angelica wrinkled her nose. 'I'd like to say that I used the three years of purgatory to learn to cook well but I'm afraid I was working so much it was invariably takeout or food at work and if I was with...you know who, he had chefs cooking for us.'

'I did a cooking course in prison.'

Angelica nearly choked on some pitta bread. Her eyes were watering but she took a sip of water before Leo had to go and pat her back. 'You...what?'

Leo nodded. 'Quite a fancy course too. I can chop vegetables like a pro and I can make an assortment of pasta dishes and slow-cooked stews. My boeuf bourguignon got special praise from the teacher.'

'That doesn't sound like it was all so bad...'

Leo made a face. 'To be perfectly honest, while it wasn't a nice environment and I learned to watch my back after I got stabbed, the worst part of it was probably the boredom. And the sense of impotency.'

He looked at her. 'The thought of you, out there with him.'

Angelica's eyes were huge. Bruised. 'I'm sorry.'

'You have nothing to be sorry for. It was all him. I boxed and did some self-defence too...to feel stronger, to be able to protect myself.'

Angelica's cheeks pinkened. 'I, er...noticed that you were a little more...muscular.'

Leo arched a brow, enjoying her embarrassment. Enjoying this whole unexpected scenario, on a tiny idyllic slice of land in the Caribbean far away from the trials and tribulations of the last few years. 'Did you, now?'

She scowled and threw an olive at him. He caught it with lightning-fast reflexes and popped it in his mouth, smiling. In fact, he felt like laughing. And he hadn't felt like laughing in a long time. Probably not since he was last with this woman.

He said, 'So tell me about this more meaningful work you want to do...'

Angelica was trying not to let her emotions get out of control but if she closed her eyes she could almost imagine that she and Leo had never broken up. It was seductive and dangerous, because they had. And then, as if that hadn't been enough, they'd been rent even further apart.

'I've been feeling for a while that I want to get out of modelling. It's a relentless business and I have no desire to be an influencer or start my own make-up or clothing line. I've been thinking about setting up some sort of charity, an outreach programme to target young people involved in areas controlled by gangs and crime, not just in Italy but all over...'

Leo popped a morsel of meat into his mouth. 'How would it work?'

'By offering a really comprehensive way out...bursaries, scholarships. A whole escape route through education with accommodation. A new life, far from their old lives.'

She went on, blossoming under Leo's intent interest. 'For instance, it was a religious charity that helped my mother to leave with my brother, but they could only afford to stay in Italy, where they would surely have been tracked down. I could afford to send them further afield, which...actually didn't work out too well in the end, because Aldo still managed to find them.'

She sat back, a little dejected. 'I don't know, maybe it's not such a great idea.'

Leo sat forward. 'Aldo had an agenda. He wanted you and so he went after information about you specifically. That's the only reason he found them. It *is* a good idea. It would take a lot of time and planning and coordination and fundraising, but it's possible. If I hadn't been sent to a foster home on the mainland through the same sort of charity that had helped your mother and brother, my life would have been very different. But you're right, at the moment it's disparate groups and the funds aren't there to give them a real, solid chance. If Aldo and I had been sent further afield, maybe to another country, who's to say that he would have stayed entangled with some elements from our home?'

'You didn't stay entangled,' Angelica pointed out.

'No, because after losing my entire family I had no illusions about how toxic that world was. My father wasn't even a big player, he'd just got into debt and couldn't pay the dues. The guy who killed them all was high on drugs, a loose cannon.'

'What a pointless waste of life...and to have witnessed that was horrific.'

Leo took a sip of wine but Angelica noticed that his hand wasn't quite steady. 'I think the only reason they didn't come after me was because I was eight.

Too young to be a threat and not important enough to chase to use, even though they were and are using kids those ages to do their dirty work.'

'My father wasn't a big player either,' confided Angelica. They'd always skirted around the specifics of what had happened in their pasts before tonight. 'He owned a shop and he'd been threatened into storing drugs and guns. A rival gang broke in and stole everything one night and he died because of that.'

Leo reached across the table and took Angelica's hand. 'I'm sorry.'

She looked at him, grief heavy in her chest. 'I'm sorry too.'

'We got out and you got your family out...they're free.'

'Yes.' Angelica let the peace of that wash over her and her heart ached for Leo's loss. So much worse than hers. She said, 'I get it, you know...'

'Get what?'

'Why you don't want to have a family. Who would want to risk that kind of trauma again?'

'Precisely.'

Angelica wanted to say more but there was a look in Leo's eye warning her off. He'd made the decision to close himself off to that risk and it wasn't up for discussion and she'd be a fool to think she could persuade him otherwise.

Obeying a rogue urge, Angelica stood up abruptly. Leo looked up at her. 'What are you doing?'

'Going for a swim.'

'It's dark.'

Angelica shrugged. She walked away from the terrace, down the garden and onto the beach. The moon was so bright, it lit up the beach and water. Then she undid the knot holding her dress up and let it drop to the ground.

She looked behind her to see where Leo had followed her to the edge of the beach. 'Coming?' She turned around and ran straight into the water and dived underneath the silky surface, telling herself that she needed to eke out every moment with Leo while they were still together because soon enough it would be over again and— A shape under the water made her squeal even though she knew it was him.

His hands went around her waist and held her. They could stand where they were—the water came up to Angelica's breasts and Leo's lower belly. His hands moved up, cupping the firm flesh, thumbs rubbing across her pebbled nipples. She sucked in a breath, hands going to his arms where his muscles bunched under her fingers.

'No more talk of the past, hm? Let's just enjoy this.'

As if she'd needed him to confirm her own thoughts.

She went close to him and wound her arms around his neck. 'Sounds like a good idea.'

'The car is here.'

Angelica sighed and turned away from the view of the iconic blue/green of the Caribbean Sea. She slipped shades over her eyes so Leo might not read how sad she was to leave this bubble behind.

They'd spent two more days in paradise, in a haze of sensual abandon, eating, drinking, swimming and sleeping. They'd been careful not to stray into the past again, keeping their conversation light and focused on the present.

And now, they were headed back to New York for a couple of days because Leo had meetings, and Angelica had a shoot booked for an iconic jewellery brand. They hadn't discussed exactly how much longer they'd continue this fake marriage but they both seemed to be tacitly agreeing not to question it. For now.

Leo was standing a few feet away in chinos and a light blue short-sleeved polo shirt that enhanced his darker tan and virile power. Muscles bulging under the short sleeves. He had lost the tight, slightly stern look he'd had since she'd seen him again.

It was as if they'd both unwound the shackles of the last three years and let them go.

'OK, I'm ready.' Angelica took a breath and filed away the memories of this idyllic hiatus, and let Leo guide her into the back of the car, his hand on her arm doing little to stop the inevitable physical reaction to his touch.

For a moment she felt panic. What if no other man ever made her feel as he did? What kind of a life would that be—always comparing someone to your first love?

Not love. It's not love, Angelica desperately told herself as they were driven to the tiny island airfield, looking out of the window in a bid to avoid looking at Leo.

But, she knew she was lying to herself. Nothing had changed. She was still in love with Leonardo Falzone.

Angelica realised that her linen trouser suit wasn't really appropriate when they arrived in New York and the temperature had dropped precipitously since they'd been here before. Winter was coming.

Leo had spent most of the flight on his phone and laptop, working. Angelica had spoken with her New York agent, who was excited about a potential opportunity for Angelica to become the face of one of the world's most famous beauty lines. Angelica knew that at the age of twenty-four, which some might consider the twilight years of her modelling career, she was incredibly lucky to still be in demand, but she told her agent she'd think about it. Signing up to a deal like that was a commitment that once she would have jumped at but which now felt constrictive.

Leo reached for her hand across the back of the car and she looked at him, forcing a smile.

He frowned. 'Hey, what's up?'

Absurdly, Angelica felt like crying, her emotions far too close to the surface. She shook her head. 'Nothing, just post-holiday blues.' She told him about the conversation with her agent.

Leo said carefully, 'Shouldn't you be looking a lot more excited? That's a massive opportunity. I've even heard of them.'

Angelica smiled for real this time. It had been an ongoing joke since they'd met that Leo hadn't the first clue about the fashion and beauty industry, not even recognising iconic designer names.

'It is, and I'm grateful for it but...it feels like a watershed moment. If I keep taking jobs like this, I'm committing to a life I'm not sure I want any more.'

Leo looked at her for a moment and then said, 'The philanthropic wing of Falzone Global Management is here in New York.' His mouth tightened. 'Needless to say, Aldo didn't have much use for them in the last few years. I could set up a meeting for you, if you like. They'd be great for advising you on how to take the next steps in creating a charity.'

A spurt of excitement filled Angelica's gut. Her eyes widened. 'Could you really? That would be amazing.'

He nodded. 'Of course, I'll do it right away. Do you want to meet them today?'

Angelica shrugged. 'Why not?'

'You can come to the office with me, then.'

'OK.' She grinned.

Leo reached out a hand and fleetingly touched her bottom lip with his thumb. 'That's better.'

Angelica's heart hitched. She brought up her hand and caught Leo's wrist and she nipped at his thumb with her teeth. His eyes flared golden. So much more golden in the last few days than that unreadable black.

He spread his hand to the back of her head and tugged her closer, dropping his mouth to hers. The kiss was slow and thorough. The kiss of a couple who had indulged for the last few days and who had relearned every inch of what they liked. It simultaneously made

Angelica's heart soar, and drop. Because she knew the end was nigh. She pulled back. They were entering Manhattan and the tall buildings soared into the sky around them.

Leo said, 'There's an event tomorrow evening at the Met museum.'

Angelica pulled back slightly. 'Do you need refined elegance or distraction from your convenient wife?'

Leo felt a punch to his gut when Angelica said *convenient wife*, even though he knew she hadn't meant it to be a dig in any way. But it just reminded him of how he'd commandeered her down the aisle, bent on revenge, and his conscience pricked.

'You know you don't have to do this, Angel. If you want to call an end to this at any time, you can.'

She tensed and drew back. 'Are you saying you don't want to be married any more?'

Leo felt another punch to his gut, one he didn't want to investigate. 'No, I'm perfectly happy with this arrangement for as long as you are. I'm conscious that you weren't given a choice at the beginning and I don't want you to feel like you still have no choice.'

She relaxed a little. 'I'm happy to be here…for now.'

Leo looked at her. She was remarkable. To have gone through the mental torture that Aldo had put her through for years and then, just when she thought she was free, to find herself being marched down the aisle again. And she'd taken it all on board with an equanimity and stoicism that shamed him. Not to mention a wicked sense of humour—wearing clothes designed to shock and provoke.

He said, 'I'm sorry that I didn't know what you'd been through. I'd never have asked you to do the things you have if I'd known.'

She suddenly looked a little shy. 'It hasn't been *all* bad.'

An image presented itself in Leo's mind, their intertwined bodies on the vast bed in the beautiful villa in the Caribbean. Pleasure coursing through his blood. Sweat cooling on their skin. And then, diving into the sea to cool off...

'No,' he agreed, feeling a little exposed. 'It hasn't been all bad, and I will make it up to you. You and your family won't have to worry about—'

Angelica put a finger to his mouth. 'You don't owe us anything, Leo. I don't regret knowing you. I'm here because I want to be.'

Before he could respond to that she said, 'I think I'll aim for refined elegance tomorrow evening. You don't need anyone to deflect attention any more, you're back.'

For the first time in Leo's life, he felt a sense of kinship, of having someone by his side who cared about what happened. He'd thought he'd had it with Aldo but, in hindsight, Aldo had always gone his own way and Leo should have seen that for what it was much earlier.

The car came to a stop outside the building housing Leo's office. 'We're here.'

Angelica suddenly looked a little concerned. 'Are

you sure it's OK to just land me in with your philanthropy team? I'm sure they're busy...'

Leo hid the little jolt he felt at her very natural and genuine concern for others. To think he'd doubted her was another shameful stain on his conscience. And yet selfishly he knew he wasn't going to take the higher road and insist on ending this marriage... If she was happy to stay for now, then he wasn't about to let her out of his sight.

'It'll be fine, they'll be only too happy to help. They've had nothing to do for the last three years and this project is one I'm willing to get behind too.'

Angelica stopped and looked up at him, eyes huge and green. 'Oh, wow, Leo, that's so kind.'

For a second Leo was oblivious to the busy Manhattan sidewalk, all he wanted to do was grab Angelica, bundle her back into the car, go straight to the apartment and recreate the magical sensual dream they'd just experienced for the last few days.

Gruffly, he said, 'It's really not kind at all. It's the least I can do.'

Angelica was still buzzing later when she got back to the apartment ahead of Leo. He was still in meetings. She'd seen him through the glass window, moving back and forth, gesticulating. She'd seen how some of the women around the boardroom table were mesmerised. And some of the men. She couldn't blame them.

He'd spotted her and had come out for a moment. He'd kissed her, in front of all of those people. An automatic and easy gesture that had almost felled her. She'd floated back down to the lobby, high on the new possibilities that her charity idea could actually work and on that kiss. Imagining for a moment—dangerously—that this could somehow be real. A real marriage. A real relationship. A partnership.

But it wasn't. They were just playacting for a little longer.

Michael, the apartment manager, was there, welcoming her back, only reinforcing that fantasy. He said, 'I'm going to go now. I've left the supplies Mr Falzone asked for in the kitchen.'

'Supplies?'

Michael nodded. 'I believe he's going to cook this evening?'

Angelica held her tongue and then said a little bemusedly, 'OK, thank you.'

When Michael had left, Angelica went into the kitchen and saw vegetables in bowls. There was meat in the fridge. And wine. Angelica groaned softly. Leo was going to cook? Was he deliberately trying to make her fall for him again?

That evening Angelica was doing her best to remain as detached as possible but it was the hardest thing she'd ever done. Leo had returned to the apartment and after disappearing to the gym for an hour or so, he'd returned and was now freshly showered and wearing soft jeans and a loose shirt, sleeves rolled up, and preparing the ingredients for a stew with professional-chef levels of competence.

Angelica was dressed in sweats and a baggy top, hair up.

Leo looked at her. 'Would you have preferred to go out to eat?'

'Not at all, this is far more entertaining.'

He looked a little embarrassed. 'I have to admit I find it relaxing.'

He'd poured her a glass of wine and she took a sip. He glanced at her. 'So tell me about the meeting with the team.'

Angelica couldn't help grinning. 'It was amazing. I mean, it was also a little scary, because, in order to really go for it, it's going to take an incredible amount of work and money…but if we can set it up properly, this could be a real game-changer for young kids and teens locked into criminal gangs, all over the world. A real lasting way out, not just being moved to a different part of the country you live in.'

She went on, 'For really young kids, born into mob families, it would have to involve a parent who might want to leave also, or being put into foster homes… and that'll take an enormous amount of resources. The government in Italy are already involved in a project to remove children from dangerous situations and so there's always a possibility of working with them.'

'Sounds like you made a lot of headway.'

'Well, thank you for letting me use your resources to see if it's a possibility.'

He looked at her. 'They're your resources too, Angel…'

She squirmed a little. 'Yes, but…we won't be married for long so...' She trailed off, not even sure if she wanted to be broaching this.

But Leo was shaking his head. 'Even if we're not married, I'd like to be the first investor of this project so you won't have to look elsewhere for initial funding or support.'

'You really don't have to do this out of a sense of—'

He held up a hand. 'Don't even say it. I'm doing this because it's a cause I believe in. I came from that background too, remember? Of course I'd love to see more kids and teens be offered a chance of another life.'

'I... OK.' Angelica felt inordinately grateful. 'That's very generous of you.'

Leo made a face. 'Aldo didn't exactly do much in the way of philanthropy while he was in charge, so it'll be good to have a worthwhile project to invest in.'

Of course Leo was thinking of the optics too, not just of easing his conscience where Angelica was concerned. That actually made her feel both better and worse at the same time. She shook her head at herself—she was being ridiculous. 'Well, thank you, we'll only go ahead with it if we think we can make it work, without putting people in danger if they leave those situations. That's the last thing we'd want.'

He looked at her. 'I'm sure you can make it work.'

Angelica felt a warm glow in her chest. It had been a long time since she'd shared aspirations and dreams with anyone.

'How are your mother and brother?'

'They're good. I'd like to see them again soon.'

'I have an invitation to a charity ball in Venice in a couple of days—you could come back to Europe with me and go see them then?'

Venice. The place where she'd first fallen for Leo and where he'd broken her heart. She hadn't been back there since. She had a feeling of foreboding that if she said yes, then maybe they'd have come full circle and both realise it was time to move on. She knew she couldn't keep going like this indefinitely. Each day it was getting harder not to drown in her own emotions.

'OK, that sounds good,' she said as lightly as she could.

Leo continued chopping and slicing his ingredients for his stew and, to save herself the mental torture of witnessing this far too appealing domestic side of Leo, Angelica muttered something about video-calling with her mother and brother and left the kitchen.

CHAPTER TEN

THE FOLLOWING EVENING Leo waited in the foyer of the Met museum for Angelica. She was coming directly from her shoot so it had made sense for them to meet here. He was at the top of the steps, having run the gauntlet of paparazzi. They'd all wanted to know where Angelica was.

A car pulled up at the bottom of the steps and, as if he could sense her, Leo went still. She'd said she would choose elegance this evening over shock value but he found he couldn't care less either way. Whatever she wore, she'd be amazing.

The back door of the car opened and one of the museum staff helped her out of the car and when Leo took her in, his legs felt weak. He knew she was a beautiful woman. But right now...she was transcendent. So much so that a hush went over the crowd. People arriving stood back, as if she were royalty. And she looked regal. Like a queen.

She was wearing a white dress. Satin, strapless. A straight sheath of material that skimmed over her curves. Her skin glowed, the after-effects of the Caribbean sun. It made Leo think about the fact that he'd noticed the sun brought out freckles across her nose.

She wore a simple diamond necklace and drop earrings. Her hair was up in an elegant chignon. She oozed sophistication and elegance and for a second Leo was almost felled by the fact that he wouldn't get to see her blossom into an even more beautiful woman as she got older. Become a mother. Work on her charity.

He didn't want that, he assured himself. That was in her future. Not his. And she deserved it. What they had now was enough. He ignored the sharp pang in his chest. In a bid to stop his mind from going down a path of investigating the fact that maybe it was too late to avoid pain, he went down the steps to meet her. And as he did, the crowd went wild. But he hardly heard them, all he could see was her, so luminously beautiful. And it wasn't just because she was physically beautiful, it shone out of her because she was a good person.

She looked at him, a mischievous glint in her eyes. 'Will I do?'

Leo felt a little choked. He nodded and managed to get out, 'You look stunning, Angel.'

Her cheeks flushed. 'Thank you, you don't look so bad yourself.'

He put out his arm and she slid hers through it. They made a striking couple, Leo in his black tuxedo and with Angelica's white dress. Eventually they made it into the event itself.

Angelica let out a breath and said a little shakily,

'I would have expected dressing formally would garner less attention.'

Leo shook his head. 'I don't think it's possible for you to go under the radar, no matter what you do.'

Sounding a little wistful, Angelica said, 'To be perfectly honest, going under the radar sounds lovely.'

Leo's conscience twinged again. As long as they were married she would be in the eye of the storm. She was tugging him forward now and they stood at the top of the stairs leading down into the crowd. He found himself tensing at the thought of being surrounded by so many people but then as if hearing his thought Angelica took her arm out of his and slid her hand into his.

He looked down at her and she said, 'Ready?'

He nodded, suddenly feeling less tense. And he noticed that, all evening, she made sure that they were never too surrounded by people, by staying close to the edges of the crowd, and orienting themselves so they were facing into the crowd rather than the other way around.

That sense of kinship was back. And he had to struggle against leaning into it. Because she was not always going to be with him. At that prospect though, instead of feeling a sense of relief or *rightness* Leo felt winded, as if someone had just punched him in the gut.

But it couldn't be any other way. He could not have this woman in his life and not be crippled with fear that he'd lose her. He had to let her go.

'OK? Do you want to move?'

Leo realised they'd moved more into the centre of the crowd but he was OK with that. *As long as she's by your side.* He looked down at her and all she could see were those huge pools of green. He had a moment of déjà vu to shortly before they'd broken up when he'd felt panicked that she seemed to have such a hold over him. And then she'd told him she loved him.

He sucked in a breath and forced himself to be rational. That was a long time ago. As she'd said herself, she'd been infatuated, and maybe he had too. But that was all. And now…it was just about chemistry and making the most out of this marriage for both of them.

He shook his head. 'No, I'm fine.'

Angelica squeezed his hand and Leo had the very sick sense that he wasn't fine at all.

Two days later

There was a knot in Angelica's gut as the water-taxi made its way up the iconic Grand Canal of Venice, to where Leo's apartment was situated, in one of the majestic palazzos lining the canal.

They pulled in at the landing jetty and Leo jumped out athletically before turning to give a hand to Angelica. She was wearing wide jeans, silk T-shirt and a light cropped jacket.

Leo led her into the reception area of the palazzo where the concierge greeted Leo with genuine affection, telling him he was so glad that Leo had been exonerated. It made Angelica feel emotional too.

Leo's apartment was on the second floor and took up the entire space. Parquet flooring and ornate original features. Oriental rugs. Soft, comfortable furnishings and coffee tables groaning under books on art and photography. When she'd been with Leo three years ago, he'd used to spend almost as much time here as in Rome.

If Angelica wasn't booked on a job, she'd used to curl up here while Leo was working in his office and flick through the books.

When they walked in she noticed something—empty spaces on the walls. 'Where are your paintings?'

Leo had been building up a small curated collection with an art broker from New York.

'Aldo took them because they were pretty much the only thing he could lift easily from the apartment. Luckily this was entirely in my name so he couldn't get his hands on it.'

Angelica shook her head. 'Unbelievable. If I'd known I would have tried to stop him, but I never came here with him.' And she was so thankful for that. As painful as some of the memories were here, she didn't need Aldo adding to the pain.

'It's fine. Faye Holt, the art broker, is doing a great job of retrieving them for me.'

'I'm glad.' There had been one she'd loved, by Matisse.

Leo looked at his watch. He was in a three-piece suit and, even after a transatlantic flight, he looked mouth-wateringly vital and gorgeous.

'I have to go to a meeting for the afternoon, but I want to show you something first…if it's here,' Leo said enigmatically.

Angelica followed him out of the living area and into the corridor where the bedrooms were. In the main bedroom, that had a small balcony/terrace overlooking the canal, Leo reached for a clothes bag that was hanging in the wardrobe. He took it out and laid it on the bed and pulled down the zip, revealing shimmering gold and chiffon and lace and silk. A dress. Ethereally beautiful, with delicate capped sleeves and a low bodice.

'What's this for?'

'The event tonight. It's a masked ball.'

Angelica noticed the feathered matching mask, attached to the dress.

He said, 'I know you can dress yourself but I took the liberty of having a stylist organise a dress.'

Angelica reached out and touched the material. 'It's beautiful, of course I'll wear it.'

'What will you do for the afternoon?'

Angelica looked at Leo. 'Actually, I have a Zoom meeting with the philanthropic team to talk about plans for the charity.'

'Great...well, if you need anything just text me.'

'I will.'

Leo looked at her for an unnervingly long time until Angelica felt herself blushing. 'What are you doing?'

Leo shook his head as if he was coming out of a trance. 'You mesmerise me.'

Angelica rolled her eyes, and held up her hand. 'We're married, Leo, you don't have to say those kinds of things to me.' *Especially when we both know that you'll undoubtedly be saying something similar to the next lover you bring here.*

Leo came close and touched Angelica's jaw. 'I've never said anything like that to another woman and I don't intend to.'

Angelica's insides twisted. 'Leo, stop, you really don't have to—'

He cut her off by swooping down and placing his mouth over hers, igniting an immediate fire between them. *Ignite?* Who was she kidding? The fire never seemed to go out.

She was clutching his shirt to stay standing when he finally broke the kiss. Angelica was breathing harshly. 'What was that for?'

Leo said, 'I can't imagine not wanting you, Angel... you're part of my blood.'

She felt shaky. Was Leo finally admitting that perhaps he could feel something more permanent for her? 'Me too.'

He straightened up. 'As much as I'd like to stay here and exorcise this fever, I can't.' He went to the door, and looked back. 'See you later?'

Angelica just nodded, her heart still pounding, skin hot. He disappeared and Angelica sank back onto the bed. Leo had just given her something with one hand and taken it away with the other. *He wanted to exorcise her from his blood.* Not admit that she might mean more to him.

Nothing had changed. If she told him she still loved him, he would surely end it all over again. Exactly as he had before. Full circle. It was nothing that Angelica didn't know and she had to dampen down the flame of hope that she was confusing with desire, or she really would never recover.

Stepping into the ballroom of the palazzo just a bit further down the Grand Canal from Leo's apartment was like stepping back in time. Flaming lanterns and massive candles lit the space in a golden glow.

Leo and Angelica were relatively restrained in their choice of clothes compared to some of the guests in full medieval-style costume with elaborate masks to match.

Leo wore a classic black tuxedo, and the stunning gold dress fitted Angelica like a dream. The matching mask sat over her eyes and she quite liked not being instantly recognisable.

Wait staff moved through the crowd with glasses of sparkling wine and canapés.

'I see someone who I need to speak to, on the other side of the room.' Leo was taking Angelica's hand and leading her through the crowd. She noticed that he seemed far more comfortable in crowds now. And, as they approached the person he wanted to talk to, he let her hand go. He introduced them and Angelica smiled politely but she soon found that Leo was engrossed in his conversation. *He didn't need her any more.*

Whatever advantage she might have brought to him in his initial phase of relaunching his business, it was well and truly expired now. And soon he would realise that and waste no time in casting her off. Albeit, salving his conscience by helping her with her charity project.

Angelica felt a pang. That wasn't fair—she was sure that Leo meant it when he said he was interested in the charity, but suddenly Angelica wasn't so sure if she wanted to have any involvement with his company, potentially having to deal with him, or see him.

But could she now jeopardise work on the charity just to make things easier for herself?

'Sorry, I didn't mean to exclude you.'

Angelica blinked out of her spiralling thoughts to see that Leo's acquaintance had moved on. She shook her head. 'It's fine. I know these things are networking opportunities.'

'Maybe you'll be back here hosting a charity event of your own soon?'

You. Not we. Another death knell. Angelica smiled. 'Maybe.'

'Dance with me.'

Angelica felt like pulling free and leaving, getting into a water-taxi and going straight to the airport. A decisive clean break. But Leo was holding her hand and the surroundings were seductive enough to believe that maybe the world outside wasn't waiting for her to start over again. Just yet. Would one more night be so selfish?

'OK.'

Leo led the way through the crowd to where couples were dancing to a mellow jazz band. He swung Angelica into his arms and she hated the way she fitted so easily. *Like coming home.* No. Coming home would be when she bought a place near to where her mother and brother lived in Madrid. She would set herself up there, and continue to work until the charity became more solid. And then she would worry about fundraising.

'Where are you?' he asked.

Angelica swallowed the emotions threatening to strangle her and forced a smile. 'Nowhere, sorry.'

Leo stopped dancing. 'Do you want to go?'

'But we just got here. Don't you have more people to meet?'

Leo shrugged. 'Not especially. Everyone knows I'm back now.'

'I'm really pleased for you, Leo.' Those damned emotions were rising again.

'Come on, let's go.'

Angelica let him lead her out, grateful for the chance to get herself back under control, and hopefully stay that way for a few more hours. *One more night*.

They were in a water-taxi on the Grand Canal within minutes. The night air was crisp and cool and Angelica huddled into her faux-fur wrap. Leo put his arm around her and pulled her into his side, and guiltily, storing up every little moment, Angelica revelled in it.

Far too soon they were back at the palazzo housing Leo's apartment. They walked up the jetty and Angelica's dress swirled around her legs in the breeze.

When they were back in the apartment, Leo pulled

off his bow tie and opened a top button. 'Would you like a nightcap?'

Angelica never really drank much but for once she fancied something. 'Sure, maybe a little watered-down whiskey?'

Leo raised a brow. 'Going straight for the hard stuff?'

'Why not?' she said lightly, shucking off the faux fur and pulling off the mask, laying them on a nearby chair.

Leo came back with two glasses and handed her one. He'd taken off his mask too. They clinked glasses and Angelica took a sip. She wandered over to the windows that looked out onto the canal and opened them, standing out on the small balcony.

Water taxis caused waves down below and a couple of gondolas meandered in their wake, couples ensconced in the back, snuggled into one another. Just as she and Leo had been. How many of these couples were on the verge of ending? She felt incredibly melancholic for a moment.

From behind her Leo said, 'Angel...'

She turned around and Leo was across the room. He put down his glass and said, 'Come here.'

A spurt of rebelliousness made her say, 'Please.'

His mouth quirked. 'Please.'

It was as if an invisible wire connected them. She was no more capable of disobeying his command than she was of denying herself breath. She lifted one foot at a time and picked off the high-heels sandals and dropped them to the floor.

As she walked towards him she reached behind her and found the zip, pulling it down. The dress loosened around her chest and when she got to within a couple of feet of Leo she pulled the small cap sleeves off her shoulders and down her arms, and then the front of the dress, revealing her breasts.

She watched his eyes widen and flare as she tugged the dress over her hips and down her legs, stepping out of the mound of gold silk and lace. Now she wore only her underpants. She reached up to her hair and pulled out the pin holding it in place so it fell down around her shoulders, almost touching her breasts.

She felt something very primal about coming to stand before him like this. As if she was presenting herself for his final delectation. She hadn't told him that she knew this was the last time they'd ever be together. Her conscience pricked but she pushed it down. They didn't owe each other anything after tonight.

Leo stepped forward and thrust his hands into her hair, tipping her face up to his. 'You are...*everything*,' he breathed.

Angelica smiled tremulously. 'Kiss me, Leo.'

He did, covering her mouth with his and sending her thoughts scattering. *Good.* She didn't want to think any more, she wanted to indulge in this night and savour every second.

Leo picked her up and carried her into the bedroom. Under the shaft of moonlight shining through the window, he stripped off his own clothes until he was naked. Angelica ogled him shamelessly, coming up on one elbow, her gaze travelling over his chest, abdominals, to his narrow waist and to where the thrusting power of him made her mouth water.

'Lie back.'

She did, and he hooked his fingers into her underwear and pulled it down and off. Leo put his hands on her legs and smoothed his way up, to her thighs and higher, pushing her legs apart as he did, exposing her to his dark golden gaze.

He came down on his knees on the floor at the end of the bed and then he proceeded to press his mouth against the inside of her legs as he came closer and closer to the juncture where her legs met.

Angelica's hands were clutching at the sheets, trying to find something to hold onto as Leo's warm breath against her sensitive skin made her skin break into goosebumps.

He pushed her legs even further apart and Angelica's breath came fast and shallow. She felt utterly exposed and yet unconcerned. She could feel the delicious abrasion of Leo's stubble against her inner thigh.

And then his mouth was there. On her. His tongue exploring her with a thoroughness that made her back arch off the bed. He reached up a hand as if to soothe her, passing over her midriff and finding a breast, squeezing the firm flesh and trapping a nipple between two fingers and squeezing, causing a sharp burst of pleasure to arrow all the way down to his wicked tongue.

The man was remorseless, ignoring Angelica's breathless pleas for mercy, until she felt herself tightening all over, hovering on the precipice before hurtling over the edge into wave after wave of pleasure so intense, she tried to put her legs together, but Leo wouldn't let her, keeping his mouth on her until she was spent and silent, breathing as if she'd just done a marathon.

She hadn't even realised her hands were in his hair and she was gripping his head. She took them away. 'I'm sorry...'

He came up over her body, grinning. 'Don't be.'

Angelica's heart spasmed. He looked so much younger and carefree. She scowled at him. 'You're evil.'

'I know, and I fully intend to be a lot more evil.'

Angelica reached for his shoulders and somehow, gathering strength into her jelly limbs, she pushed him so that he fell onto his back on the bed. She pressed him down and said, 'Not so fast.'

Leo was unperturbed. He put his arms behind his head, reminding her of how he'd gained her trust by letting her restrain him. Another heart spasm. She should have known to trust him from the start...but then they wouldn't have had all of this...

She started pressing kisses to his chest, finding the flat disc of a nipple and teasing it with her tongue. She put a hand on his lower belly, feeling the muscles contract, and explored further, circling his erection with one hand as she made her way down and down until he was now rigid with tension.

Taking her time, she let her hand explore his stiff flesh, feeling how the skin slipped up and down over the shaft, and then, when she could see perspiration on his brow, she bent forward and put her mouth around him.

Madre de Dio...he was going to die right here on this bed. And he knew if he did he would die happy. Angelica was a sorceress, taking him to a place he'd never been before, because he usually didn't like lovers performing oral sex on him—until Angelica, that was. He'd always felt too exposed. But the first time she'd done it to him, back when they'd first got together, it had been so innocent and obvious that she hadn't known what she was doing that he'd given into the temptation, and now...he'd created a monster.

She was as merciless as he had just been, pushing him over the edge before he could stop himself, taking all of him, and then sliding back up his body, with those soft curves, and a smile like the Cheshire Cat.

Leo hauled her up all the way. They were glued together. He cupped her bottom and then gave one cheek a playful slap. 'You'll pay for that.'

'Promises, promises.'

She put her head down, into the place where his shoulder met his neck, her breath feathering over his skin. A feeling of intense peace washed over Leo, the kind of peace he'd never thought he'd experience again.

He ran his hand lazily up and down Angelica's back, letting himself recover, and then he heard a gentle snore and smiled, letting that sense of peace lull him into joining her.

CHAPTER ELEVEN

WHEN LEO WOKE the next morning he felt both amazingly relaxed and hungover. But not from drink. A sex hangover. Images filled his head. After he and Angelica had initially fallen asleep, they'd woken again a while later, filled with mutual hunger. A hunger that had bordered on desperation sometimes.

They'd finally fallen asleep again around dawn. And now... Leo cracked open his eyes. The sun was high outside. And the bed was empty beside him. He put out an arm. It was cold.

He came up on one elbow, feeling as if he'd missed his footing even though he was lying down. He threw back the covers and got up, heading straight for the shower. Afterwards he pulled on the first things to hand, jeans and a loose shirt, a niggling sense of unease trickling down his spine.

He went out into the main part of the apartment and for a second didn't notice anything but then he saw her. She was standing at the open windows, looking out onto the canal.

She was dressed in the jeans she'd worn the previous day, sneakers and a sweatshirt. Hair pulled back in a ponytail. She looked ridiculously young. Then he noticed the suitcase beside her and her handbag, across her body.

The unease intensified. Maybe she'd got booked for a job. 'Angel?'

She turned around and Leo noticed that she was pale and her face was set. She also had shadows under her eyes but then that wasn't a surprise. They hadn't had much sleep.

Trying not to let the unease show in his voice, he said, 'Are you going somewhere?'

She nodded. 'I'm afraid I've been lying to you, Leo, and myself a little bit too.'

He frowned. 'What do you mean?' Suddenly he felt cold, thinking that perhaps all this time, when he'd believed in her story, maybe he'd missed an even bigger agenda...

Oblivious to his cynical mind whirring into action again, she said, 'The truth is that I still love you, Leo. I never stopped. I convinced myself I had, or that it hadn't been love, but it was a lie.'

She shrugged minutely and tried to force a smile but Leo could see the emotion in her eyes and, like a coward, he would have preferred in that moment that perhaps she had been lulling him into a false sense of security for some nefarious end. This was far more threatening. He could feel himself closing off, shutting down.

She said, 'Believe me, I get the irony of being back in more or less exactly the same spot having the same conversation, three years later.' She let out a short harsh laugh that didn't sound like her at all. 'You'd think I'd have learnt by now.'

'I didn't give you much choice,' Leo had to concede. 'I dragged you back into my life.'

He said now, 'Angel... I'm sorry I can't say what you want to hear. It's not something I've ever wanted in my life...a lifetime commitment, family.' So why did the words feel like ash on his tongue?

He noticed her throat working as she swallowed. 'I think the worst of it is that I understand, because I lost someone too. And I grew up surrounded by the threat of violence all the time.'

'But...this is the thing...none of us are guaranteed a life without pain, or loss. Some experience more than most, granted...but do you not see that by choosing to close yourself off to the risk of losing anyone ever again, you're doing a disservice to the memory of your parents? And your brothers?'

A red mist of pain came over Leo's vision. 'It's precisely why I can't have what they never experienced.'

'Just because you survived, it doesn't mean that you have to forgo love and happiness in your own life. I know you don't love me, but some day you might meet someone and you deserve to be happy, Leo, you're a good man and you've created something worth sharing. It can be very lonely closing yourself off. I did it for three years to survive that marriage and it almost killed me.'

Leo couldn't think straight. He felt a multitude of things all at once. Panic. 'What will you do? Where will you go?'

Angelica looked resigned. Sad. He had done that to her. He'd also made her laugh and sigh and moan and—

'I'll go to Madrid. I think I'll buy a place there, to be near Mama and Paolo. Then I'll continue working while getting the charity up and running, and then, hopefully some day soon, retire from modelling and work full time on that.'

'And what about the rest of your life?' Leo wondered why he was asking her this. He had no right. He should let her go.

She hitched up her chin. 'I want love, Leo. And I want a family. I want to bring up kids in an environment where they won't feel threatened. Of course there's no guarantee of peace and safety anywhere but some places are better than others. I want to be happy. Fulfilled.'

Those sentiments hit Leo hard. He thought of how it had affected him to see happy families—abject fear. 'You will be. You'll be an amazing mother and wife. And philanthropist. You'll change lives. You deserve to be happy, Angel.' Again, the words were like ash, souring his tongue.

'Thank you. I have something for you.'

She came towards him and held out a chain. It took him a second to register what was on it. A Murano glass heart, green, gold and orange, and her engagement ring and wedding ring.

He held out his palm and she dropped them into it. His head was full of the memory of her spotting that little glass heart in the window of a shop three years ago and how he'd immediately wanted to give it to her, so he'd gone in and bought it.

'I can't believe you still have it.'

'I kept it. But it's yours. And the rings are yours too. I donated the one Aldo gave me to charity, maybe you can do the same with these.'

Angelica had gone over to pick up her case and was walking to the door of the apartment before Leo came out of the past. He turned around. He felt as if he were under water, or watching her through glass. He wasn't even sure if she'd hear him if he called her name.

She stopped at the door and then, as if deciding not to say anything, she opened it and then she was gone. She didn't even look back.

Much like the day when she'd walked out that first time, he had an instinct to run after her. But how could he when he couldn't give her what she wanted?

Leo stood there for a long moment, with the necklace and rings in his hand. He looked at them stupidly. The heart seemed to glow, as if to mock him. *You have no heart.* No. It stopped beating the day his family lost their lives.

But he could feel it now, thumping heavily. As heavy as the stone in his gut. And the boulder in his chest. He felt very tired all of a sudden, as if he'd been trying to roll a ball up a hill for ever and it had just rolled down again, flattening him in the process. What was the name of that Greek king? Sisyphus?

Without really thinking, Leo went over to where Angelica had been standing at the window and looked out, and down. There was a water-taxi, and the driver was helping her in. She was wearing sunglasses and facing forward but he knew she was crying.

He'd made her cry. More than once. He'd also unwittingly fed her to Aldo, who had been so jealous of anything Leo loved that he'd wanted her for himself.

Leo's hand closed over the necklace and rings as that word resounded in his head. *Love. Loved. Love.*

Things were falling into place now, like pieces of a jigsaw. How out of it he'd been after Angelica had left—*after you rejected her.* How easy it had been for Aldo to take advantage of Leo's distraction.

Because Aldo had seen what not even Leo had seen. That he'd fallen in love with Angelica.

Of course he had. She'd turned his life upside down and inside out and he hadn't been able to handle it. So he'd rejected her rather than face the fact that he was a coward and too scared to seize love when it was gifted to him.

He looked down again to see the water-taxi pulling away from the landing pier, joining the traffic of the other water-taxis, boats and gondolas on the busy canal.

And suddenly, Leo knew that Angelica was right. About everything. What had she said? *I know you don't love me.* He'd fallen in love with her the moment he'd laid eyes on her.

He stuffed the necklace and rings in his pocket and ran.

Angelica couldn't even hide her sobs. She wondered how many women this water-taxi had ferried up the canal, sobbing noisily in the back, tears streaming under their black shades. The driver was ignoring her anyway, so presumably it wasn't that uncommon.

She was standing in the back of the boat, hanging onto the railing, calling herself all kinds of a fool for letting herself be hurt by the same man twice.

It took Angelica a minute to hear it over her crying and the engine and the general noises on the canal but then she heard, 'Angel! Stop!'

She looked around and had to lift her shades up to see better. In another water-taxi, closing in on them fast, was Leo, jumping up and down and gesticulating. He looked crazed. Angelica's mouth fell open.

The boat came alongside hers and Leo was shouting instructions to the driver to get closer. He stood up on the edge of the boat and Angelica squealed, 'What are you doing? You'll fall in!'

Leo braced himself and then leapt the short distance between the bobbing boats, landing in the back and almost toppling over. Angelica reached for him, catching him. She looked down. 'Your feet are bare!'

He'd run out straight after her? A tiny seed of hope bloomed in her chest. Leo caught her arms and glanced away for a moment to say something to the driver. Angelica didn't even register what, she couldn't look away from him.

He looked at her. She shook her head. 'What are you doing?'

'Am I too late?'

'For what?'

'To come with you.'

'Where?'

'Wherever you go, for ever.'

Angelica put a hand to her mouth to swallow a little sob. The tears kept coming. She shook her head. 'No, you're not too late. But...what are you saying, Leo?'

He smiled and wiped at her tears with his thumbs. 'I never want to be the cause of your tears again. What I'm saying, *amore mio*, is that I love you. I've always loved you but I was too scared to admit it, and we paid an awful price for my cowardice.'

Angelica turned her face into Leo's hand, kissing his palm. She looked up at him. 'It wasn't cowardice, it was self-protection.'

'You're right, by choosing to cut myself off from you, from love, I'm insulting the memory of my family. They deserve better, *I* deserve better, and you definitely deserve better. But...do you really want me? After all I've put you through?'

'You have to ask me that? I love you, Leo. I never stopped. I want to have a family with you and grow old with you and see our grandchildren turn into adults.'

Leo's eyes shone suspiciously. 'I'll do my best. It might take me a while to get used to the notion. I used to have panic attacks when I saw happy families.'

Angelica interlaced her fingers with his. 'We'll go as slowly as it takes, my love, and before you even realise what's happening, we'll be a family.'

Leo kissed her as they swayed with the motion of the boat. Unbeknownst to them they had become surrounded by sightseers and paparazzi who regularly trawled the canal looking for celebrities.

The pictures of Leo and Angelica kissing passionately went viral. As did the pictures of him placing a Murano heart around her neck, and rings on her finger. Speculation was rife as to what had happened but there was no doubt, as the boat turned and went back to the palazzo, that they were very much in love and happy.

In fact, their obvious passion and love inspired a well-known designer to offer them an extortionate amount of money to appear in an ad campaign together, which Leo only agreed to once all the proceeds went to Angelica's new charity.

EPILOGUE

A MONTH AFTER their viral boat moment, they were back in Venice to renew their vows with a formal blessing. With the bride in full agreement this time. Angelica wore a whimsical white ruffled gown and an antique lace veil, with a bouquet of assorted seasonal flowers.

Paolo, who'd brought his girlfriend, walked Angelica down the aisle and her mother was there too, with her boyfriend. Fully reunited, safe and happy. Angelica was grateful every day for that fact.

And then, three years later, they were back in Venice on a holiday break. As they walked down the narrow streets, something caught Leo's attention out of the corner of his eye and he stopped and faced a window.

In the reflection he could see himself with a two-year-old boy, his son, Luca, on his shoulders. Angelica was beside him, eating a gelato, and handing it up to Luca to take a bite. Strapped to her front in a papoose was their newest arrival, their baby daughter, Sara.

She'd told him it would happen without him even realising it, and it had. They were a family. And sometimes it terrified him, but mostly it gave him an immense amount of pride and love and awe. And hope.

He looked down at her and smiled. She saw their reflection in the window and she smiled too, because she *knew*.

She slipped her hand into his and they carried on their way, just one more family among the many others. Maybe a little more in love, and maybe a little bit happier, because of the journey it had taken for them to come back together again. For ever.

* * * * *

Did you fall in love with Bride of Betrayal?
Then make sure to catch up on
these other dramatic stories
by Abby Green!

"I Do" For Revenge
The Heir Dilemma
On His Bride's Terms
Rush to the Altar
Billion-Dollar Baby Shock

Available now!

Get up to 4 Free Books!

We'll send you 2 free books from each series you try PLUS a free Mystery Gift.

FREE Value Over **$25**

Both the **Harlequin Presents** and **Harlequin Medical Romance** series feature exciting stories of passion and drama.

YES! Please send me 2 FREE novels from Harlequin Presents or Harlequin Medical Romance and my FREE gift (gift is worth about $10 retail). After receiving them, if I don't wish to receive any more books, I can return the shipping statement marked "cancel." If I don't cancel, I will receive 6 brand-new larger-print novels every month and be billed just $7.19 each in the U.S., or $7.99 each in Canada, or 4 brand-new Harlequin Medical Romance Larger-Print books every month and be billed just $7.19 each in the U.S. or $7.99 each in Canada, a savings of 20% off the cover price. It's quite a bargain! Shipping and handling is just 50¢ per book in the U.S. and $1.25 per book in Canada.* I understand that accepting the 2 free books and gift places me under no obligation to buy anything. I can always return a shipment and cancel at any time. The free books and gift are mine to keep no matter what I decide.

Choose one: ☐ **Harlequin Presents Larger-Print** (176/376 BPA G36Y)   ☐ **Harlequin Medical Romance** (171/371 BPA G36Y)   ☐ **Or Try Both!** (176/376 & 171/371 BPA G36Z)

Name (please print)

Address   Apt. #

City   State/Province   Zip/Postal Code

Email: Please check this box ☐ if you would like to receive newsletters and promotional emails from Harlequin Enterprises ULC and its affiliates. You can unsubscribe anytime.

Mail to the **Harlequin Reader Service:**
IN U.S.A.: P.O. Box 1341, Buffalo, NY 14240-8531
IN CANADA: P.O. Box 603, Fort Erie, Ontario L2A 5X3

Want to explore our other series or interested in ebooks? Visit www.ReaderService.com or call 1-800-873-8635.

---

*Terms and prices subject to change without notice. Prices do not include sales taxes, which will be charged (if applicable) based on your state or country of residence. Canadian residents will be charged applicable taxes. Offer not valid in Quebec. This offer is limited to one order per household. Books received may not be as shown. Not valid for current subscribers to the Harlequin Presents or Harlequin Medical Romance series. All orders subject to approval. Credit or debit balances in a customer's account(s) may be offset by any other outstanding balance owed by or to the customer. Please allow 4 to 6 weeks for delivery. Offer available while quantities last.

Your Privacy—Your information is being collected by Harlequin Enterprises ULC, operating as Harlequin Reader Service. For a complete summary of the information we collect, how we use this information and to whom it is disclosed, please visit our privacy notice located at https://corporate.harlequin.com/privacy-notice. Notice to California Residents – Under California law, you have specific rights to control and access your data. For more information on these rights and how to exercise them, visit https://corporate.harlequin.com/california-privacy. For additional information for residents of other U.S. states that provide their residents with certain rights with respect to personal data, visit https://corporate.harlequin.com/other-state-residents-privacy-rights/.